MURDER WEARS A MASK

A KELLY ARMELLO COZY MYSTERY BOOK 1

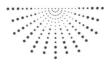

DONNA DOYLE

D1523225

CONTENTS

DIFFERENT RULES

"**H**old on there, Troy!"

Officer Troy Kennedy, his ticket pad and pen in hand, looked up from the parking meter which indicated that the time had run out. Officer Kyle Moore approached on his motorized scooter. Kyle's physical handicap prevented him from following the usual routine of his fellow officers, but no one was more zealous in issuing parking tickets to the cars who had overstayed the meter. Why Kyle would suddenly prove reluctant to see one issued this time was a puzzle, and Troy's expression showed this.

"You can't ticket that car," Kyle told him when he came closer.

"Who says I can't?" Troy pointed to the lapsed time on the meter. "It's out of minutes."

"But that's Scotty Stark's car," Kyle said as if this were sufficient reason.

"Who's Scotty Stark?"

"He's Chief Stark's son, that's who. And the mayor's nephew. The chief is married to the mayor's sister, Lois."

"Okay," Troy said, dismissive of the Settler Springs family genealogy. "But the car is out of time."

"He probably stopped to visit his dad before heading back to college," Kyle said. "The meter probably just ran out."

"No, it didn't just run out. The car was here an hour ago when I passed, and it was already out of time. I figured I'd give the guy a break then and check again when I came back through. I didn't know who owns the car. Nice car. How's a college kid get a car like this?"

"Now you know who owns the car," Kyle said, ignoring the question.

"If I'd known it was the chief's son," Troy went on, "I'd have gone into the station to let him know he needed to move his car."

Kyle shook his head. "That's not how it goes, Troy," he said, sounding as if he were instructing a novice. "Scotty Stark's car doesn't get a ticket. You know the mayor's family's cars don't get ticketed. You let me handle this."

"I've already written the ticket," Troy said, irritated at Kyle's tone. He wasn't a novice. He'd served two deployments in Afghanistan and was still a member of the National Guard. He didn't need to be told how to do his job.

"Take my advice, son," Kyle said. "Tear it up." He leaned over from his perch on the motorized scooter and pulled the ticket free from the red car's windshield. He handed it to Troy. "Tear it up."

The two men locked gazes; Troy's eyes were blue and defiant; Kyle's were brown, patient and resigned. "Tear it up, son," Kyle said again. "Trust me."

"Kyle—"

"It's the way things are in Settler Springs," Kyle said. "You'll learn that if you haven't already. You're new in town. But the Starks and the Truverts run the town." His weathered face broke into a grin. "And the Krymanskis break the laws. You keep those two facts straight and you'll come out okay."

Troy didn't bother to protest. He put the crumpled ticket into his pocket and, with a curt nod of farewell to Kyle, walked to the squad car and got in. His shift was over, and he was ready for it to end. After a night that had included a domestic abuse arrest and a drug overdose, Kyle's concern for a parking ticket was more than he was able to tolerate. It was time to go home and try to do some studying before he went back on duty. He was working tonight, filling in for Officer Leo Page, who needed the evening off because he was taking his grandchildren trick-or-treating for Halloween. Leo was a good guy; he and his wife were raising their grandchildren because their daughter was in rehab again and their son-in-law was in prison. It was guys like Leo who deserved breaks, not the police chief's son.

It was Halloween. Troy knew to expect some rowdiness tonight. A warm autumn had gotten the pranksters off to an early start. The kids, one of them a Krymanski, had been engaging in the usual Halloween vandalism since the month began. Some of it wasn't so bad; handfuls of Indian corn thrown on porches, pumpkins smashed, trees wrapped in toilet paper. But when a group of kids threw eggs at the mayor's house, that was different. Troy had found out that when there was trouble of that nature, it was usually quicker to find out what the Krymanskis had been doing that night.

There were different branches of the black sheep Krymanskis in Settlers Springs. It turned out that fourteen-year old Lucas Krymanski had been the culprit behind the egging of the mayor's house. Tia Krymanski, a single mother with five children, tried to keep a tight leash on her brood which was why their run-ins with the law didn't extend to the more serious violations of other branches of the Krymanski family. Lucas had paid for his sins; in addition to having to do community service hours at the public library, his mother had grounded him, and for two weeks, he went to school, then to the library, and then home. When Tia Krymanski was riled up, her children knew better than to cross her, and Lucas had borne his punishment meekly.

But the two weeks were up, and he wasn't grounded anymore. In Lucas's eyes, that meant that he was free to enjoy the pleasures of Halloween, even if his mother had told him that, at age fourteen, he was too old to go out trick-or-treating. Loathe to abstain from the prospect of free candy, Lucas had already made plans to meet his friends at 6:30, when trick-or-treating started. They would don masks and go from house to house for candy. Some townspeople, who were generous when petite Disney princesses and miniature Paw Patrol characters came to the door, would scowl at the oversize, overage youths, but others would smile good-naturedly and throw candy in the pillowcases that the boys used for trick-or-treat bags.

Trick-or-treating ended at 8:30. Mom wouldn't be off work until 9:30 after she finished at the restaurant. By that time, Lucas would be home, his pillowcase back on his bed, his candy safely hidden away, and the evidence of his transgression concealed from his mother's vigilant eyes.

His older sister Carrie met him on the stairs as he was on his way inside after finishing his community service hours at the library. "Mom left mac and cheese for you in the oven," she said.

"Uh-huh," he answered.

"Don't go trick-or-treating," she warned. At seventeen and the eldest of Tia Krymanski's children, Carrie had what Lucas considered an annoying tendency to act like she was the boss of the family when Mom wasn't around.

"Where are you going?" Lucas countered.

He knew he had her when she hesitated. She was probably going out to meet her boyfriend. Mom didn't allow Carrie to go out on school nights, but Lucas guessed that his sister planned to capitalize on Mom being at work, just like he was.

"I'm studying," she said.

"At the library?"

"No, with friends," she replied, knowing that his hours of community service meant that he could easily ask Miss Armello, the librarian, if his sister had been at the library after he left. "Don't go trick-or-treating."

But there was no strength in her warning. The two of them were bonded together in a sibling code of silence. She wouldn't tell if he wouldn't.

Lucas raced into the house. He headed first to the kitchen; if Mom came home and the macaroni and cheese wasn't eaten, she'd know he hadn't stayed home. He wolfed down the meal; it was homemade, not the box mix that was made with powdered cheese. Mom knew how to cook, which was why she worked so many hours at The Corner Café, whose menu boasted meals that were made the way Grandma used to make them.

Lucas remembered to rinse out the casserole dish; Mom yelled when they just left the dirty dishes in the sink for her to wash. He didn't want to give her any reason to be in a bad temper when she got home. He didn't foresee any likelihood that she would discover that he had disobeyed her instructions not to go trick-or-treating, but it was best to be cautious. His Darth Vader mask would cover his face so that no one could tell who he was. He would be dressed in jeans and a tee shirt like most of the other kids his age who were also protesting the belief that Halloween was for little kids, making it unlikely that anyone would recognize him and tell his mother that he had been out. He was using the pillowcase that was on his bed, so there would be no missing linens from the bathroom cupboard.

None of his siblings would see him leave. The eight-year-old twins, Alexa and Madison, had gone home on the bus with their friend Taylor; they would be trick-or-treating in her neighborhood that night. Twelve-year old Marissa, conscious of her status as a seventh-grader, would not have dreamed of going trick-or-treating like the little kids. She was helping out at the Café because, although she was too young to have working papers, the owner, Mr. Caputo, paid her under the table to wash dishes.

Lucas left his bedroom light on, the kitchen light on, and the living room light on. If anyone drove by, they would see that someone must be home because the lights were on. His mom always yelled at the kids for leaving the lights on, but that was preferable to her suspecting that he wasn't home. It was important to choose misdeeds according to rank. Lucas was wise to the ways of discipline. It was Halloween, and he had everything planned.

2

THE BODY IN THE ALLEY

Lucas had lived in Settler Springs for all of his fourteen years and there was no alley, street, cul-de-sac, or corner that had not been explored by him, either on foot or while riding his bicycle. He knew that the alley behind Laurelei's Designs, next to the parking lot of Sam Sloan's Insurance Agency, was the best meeting place. It was dark there. The businesses were closed, and no one would be inside to work or coming outside for their cars. The alleys in Settler Springs lacked streetlights and would be camouflaged by the spread of darkness and the opaque buildings. With the noise of Halloween all around, there would be no indication that anyone was using the alley for a meeting place.

Lucas wasn't surprised that Chris and Tyler were late. Tyler was always late. Chris would have to finish his homework before he was allowed out. His parents weren't strict like Mom was about trick-or-treating at age fourteen, but Chris had gotten a failing mark in English on his mid-quarter report card and his parents had warned him that he'd be grounded if he brought home a failing grade for the term.

Lucas surreptitiously turned into the alley from Roosevelt Avenue. Crowds of children, accompanied by their parents, were traveling the street, making it difficult for him to get through. He was grateful for his Darth Vader mask when he spied his seven-year old cousin, Abby Krymanski, with her parents, but they paid no attention to him as he went by. There would be plenty of Darth Vaders out tonight, he was sure; too many for anyone to notice.

After turning into the alley, the lights of the street were gone, and he was in darkness. Autumn leaves, which had fallen from the trees and not been blown away by the storm the week before, crackled beneath his sneaker-shod feet. It was the only sound in the alley, and it was appropriately creepy for Halloween. Lucas considered the many horror movies that he had watched with his friends over the years. He couldn't recall one where the sound of dry leaves crackling had been a particularly frightening setting, but still, there was something about the dark alley that made the noise seem ominous.

When he heard a car at the other end of the alley, Lucas stepped back into the protection of the building where he couldn't be seen. He heard a car door open, then a second door open. Lucas held his breath as if even that sound could put him in danger. It was just like a movie, even though he knew that the car was likely just someone coming home from work or going out to the store. Not everyone was involved in Halloween.

Something that sounded like a package being dropped broke the stillness of the night. The wind was light, sending the leaves scuttling in circles upon the pavement. The night was overcast, the half-moon invisible behind a thick wall of clouds. It felt like it was going to rain. Lucas hoped it would hold off until he and his friends had had a chance to get their share of candy before the little kids took it all.

He heard the car doors close quickly, first one, then the other. Then he saw the headlights heading his way. Lucas, safe in the calyx of darkness from the buildings, pressed himself against the wall of the insurance agency so that he couldn't be seen. The car went by too fast for him to be seen or for him to see the driver.

It didn't matter, Lucas told himself. Lots of people cut through the alleys as shortcuts. With the streets so crowded because of the kids trick-or-treating, it wasn't a surprise that someone would use the alley to avoid the traffic.

Chris and Tyler still hadn't arrived. Lucas adjusted his Darth Vader mask and zipped up his hoodie. The air was turning colder. He decided to see if they were coming from the other end of the alley and he walked in that direction. It was even darker on this end, farther from the streetlights on Roosevelt Avenue; there was only minimal illumination from a lighted pumpkin ornament hanging in the window of the tenant who lived above Olsen's Jewelry. He couldn't help but look over his shoulder as he walked, alert to any possible noise, even when it was merely the sound of the leaves dancing upon the pavement when the wind blew.

It was a long alley and darker as he walked farther along it. There weren't any people around, but that was why he and Chris and Tyler had chosen it as a meeting place. He had walked two-thirds of the way down the alley when he stumbled.

There was something on the side of the alley where he was walking. He peered down, trying to distinguish what he had bumped into, but the alley was too dark for him to discern anything. He squatted down, reaching out with his hands to find out what was in front of him.

It was something in a garbage bag. But it didn't feel like garbage.

He wished that Chris and Tyler were with him. He'd have felt better making a decision with input from his friends on what he should do next. He could just leave whatever it was right where it was, go back to the entrance to the alley and pretend that he'd never left, never heard the car stop, never heard it take off, never encountered whatever it was.

But curiosity was stronger than caution. Lucas pulled open the drawstrings for the garbage bag. It was one of the larger bags, not the yard-size bags but the bigger ones that were used by construction companies. Lucas knew about that because he had an uncle who worked construction and brought bags home when he was doing a project around the house. Mom said that was stealing, but she tended to be critical of his Krymanski relatives.

He took out his cell phone so that he could see what was in the bag after he had unknotted the drawstrings. When a Princess Leia mask stared back at him, glowing eerily against the dark garbage bag,

Lucas was so startled that he almost dropped his phone. With trepidation, he reached into the garbage bag. His hand touched something soft, but warm. It couldn't be—

Steeling himself, Lucas pulled the garbage bag lower and pointed his phone at the contents. It was a body, dressed in a Princess Leia costume. He thought she must be dead, but what if she wasn't? What if she needed help? Lucas lifted up the mask only enough to expose her neck so that he could feel for a pulse.

There was nothing. He put the mask back in place and stood up. He couldn't leave her like this, in the alley where a car could run over her. He put his phone back into his pocket and, pulling on the garbage bag, dragged it away from the road. This end of the alley wasn't busy; the back doors of several businesses that were closed after five o'clock were all that was here, and no one was likely to be going in or out.

He had to tell someone. Mom would kill him if she knew that he'd disobeyed her orders not to go trick-or-treating and ended up finding a dead body. But who could he go to? And where were Chris and Tyler?

He texted them and waited for an answer. Tyler still had to do his chores before he was allowed out. That meant at least an hour, Lucas knew. Chris was still doing his homework. He debated whether to tell his friends what he'd found but decided not to say anything. They'd think he was pranking them, most likely, and by now, Lucas was not only in no mood to prank anybody, but he didn't much feel like trick-or-treating either.

Dispiritedly, Lucas rolled up the pillowcase and stuffed it inside his hoodie. He kept the Darth Vader mask on as he walked to the end of the alley and debated which way to go. If he went right, he could go to The Café where his mom would be working in the kitchen. If he went left, he could go to the library where Miss Armello, who was costumed as Professor McGonagall of Hogwarts, would be handing out candy and bookmarks to trick-or-treaters.

Miss Armello would know what to do. And she wouldn't yell at him or ground him. He turned left.

3

HELP FROM MISS ARMELLO

K elly Armello had loved Halloween when she was a young child and trick-or-treating was a fashion show of little two-legged pumpkins and princesses, Woody, and Buzz from Toy Story. But that was before the innocence of the occasion was taken over by grotesque, macabre costumes that seemed more likely to celebrate serial killers of the silver screen than the playful characters with which she'd grown up. Keeping a healthy balance between the holiday and the endearing nature of childhood was something that took a great deal of thought when she was planning programming at the library, but when Kelly committed herself to something, she put her all into it.

The library had been decorated in orange and black since the beginning of October. Plastic pumpkins were everywhere. The circulation desk was decorated with a string of black cat lights. At the end of every shelving unit there was a cut-out figure of a smiling witch, a cheerful ghost, a goofy Frankenstein, a grinning vampire, and a werewolf so furry that he looked like he was up for adoption from an animal shelter. Of course, she included Maleficent, Ursula, and other Disney villains so that wherever patrons went in search of a book, they were welcomed by a Halloween character who had earned his or her—or its—place in the pantheon. Upstairs in the children's corner, the characters were even more benign; a poster of Ariel was glued to the door and inside, the youngest patrons were greeted by representations of Peppa Pig, a stuffed unicorn, Belle, and Mulan.

On the glass door of the library was a large drawing of a light bulb to show that the library was taking part in trick-or-treat. In case anyone was unsure of their welcome, there was a sign in front of the doors saying, "Enter if you dare—candy ahead!"

The children who were familiar with the library and its programs went in eagerly to be greeted by Miss Kelly, who marveled at their costumes, tried to guess who they were, and handed out candy from a giant bowl that seemed as if it would never run out of candy. Miss Carmela, who was dressed (appropriately, the parents thought) as a witch, stood at the desk as if she dared anyone to ask to check out a book.

Adult patrons leery of the invasion of children had already left the library, preferring to return when it was less occupied by noisy youngsters. This was the night for the children and Miss Kelly made sure that the library gave out the best candy of all the businesses in town. She paid for it herself so that no one could balk at the expense; the library building was owned by the borough, but Kelly Armello wasn't going to be reduced to handing out cheap little lollipops just to please the library board, even if Mrs. Stark, the board president, thought she should do so.

One group of ballet dancers and princesses had just left when Kelly noticed that Darth Vader was making a solo entrance. She smiled. She wasn't surprised that Lucas Krymanski was out trick-or-treating, even though he had told her he wasn't allowed. He had helped her with the decorating as part of his community service hours, and tomorrow, he'd be helping her to take everything down.

"Lucas," she greeted him. "Have some candy."

Lucas shook his head and took off the mask. "Miss Armello, can you come with me?"

"Why? What's wrong?" Lucas looked shaken and it wasn't like him to be ill-at-ease. He was a happy-go-lucky sort of a kid who reminded her of Huckleberry Finn; a little rough around the edges, but with a good heart.

"I need you to come," he said, a pleading note in his voice.

Was something wrong at home? She knew that, while the Krymanskis were notorious for being involved in everything from pranks to traffic violations to more serious offenses, Tia Krymanski, who had married into the family, was a strict mother. She wasn't one to allow her offspring to run wild. But that didn't mean that something wasn't wrong.

"Carmela, I'm going to go with Lucas. You can handle things?"

Carmela Dixon glared at Lucas. "You want me to hand out candy and wait on patrons?" she demanded. Carmela was the library assistant, not the director, and having to take orders from a young woman half her age rankled.

"Yes," Kelly said calmly. "I don't think you'll have many patrons tonight, and there's plenty of candy. I'm sure some of the parents will write letters to the board to thank us for welcoming the kids and handing out candy." That last remark was a reminder to Carmela not to be rude to the children or someone might complain.

"I'll lock up," Carmela said.

"It's not eight-thirty yet," Kelly said. "I'll be back before then."

Carmela's gaze swept over Lucas. He was a Krymanski, her expression said. Dealing with a Krymanski could take the rest of the night.

"But if I'm not," Kelly sighed, "then yes, you may lock up."

Kelly pulled on her shawl and followed Lucas out of the library. The streets were still occupied by characters in costume in search of candy. Kelly hoped that Carmela wouldn't be too unfriendly to the children.

"Lucas, where are we going?" she asked. Lucas had simply begun walking fast, dodging the throngs of trick-or-treaters as if he were in a hurry to get to his destination.

"The alley," he said.

"Lucas, what's wrong? Why are we going—what alley?"

"The one off Roosevelt Avenue."

"Daffodil Alley," Kelly said automatically. Five years ago, in an attempt to give every address a name, the borough council had named all of the alleys after flowers. No one bothered to refer to the alleys by their names, however, and Daffodil Alley remained the alley off Roosevelt Avenue.

Kelly was tall and she jogged daily, but she was having a hard time keeping up with Lucas, who was walking as if he had winged feet. She had never seen him like this, and she wondered what was so dire that he had asked her to leave the library and come with him. Lucas wasn't one inclined for theatrics. It was possible that he was planning a Halloween prank, but she doubted that. Whatever his reasons for getting her, he wasn't enjoying this.

Finally, they reached Daffodil Alley.

"It's pretty dark," Lucas said, taking out his cell phone so that they had light.

It occurred to Kelly that there wasn't much to conjure an impression of daffodils in the alley. All she could see was the outline of trash cans put out for the next day's garbage collection. The alley bore an aura of neglect, as if the back lots of the businesses needn't bother trying to keep up appearances because there was no one here who was likely to notice.

"Over there," Lucas gestured with his phone.

"Over where—how can you see anything?"

Lucas led her to the back lot of one of the businesses that was closed for the night. "Here," he said, kneeling down.

"What is it?"

"It's a garbage bag. There's a body in it."

His voice broke. He was fourteen, but this wasn't one of the signs of puberty. It was apparent that Lucas was upset. As anyone would be if they thought there was a body inside a garbage bag. But Kelly doubted that what Lucas said was true.

Someone with a macabre sense of humor had likely stuffed a dummy with newspaper, dressed it in clothing, and put it in a garbage bag to scare the kids into summoning the police. It was a joke. A joke in poor taste, to be sure, and not one that would make the police happy.

Lucas was unfastening the opening of the garbage bag. Gently, he lowered the flaps and lifted his cell phone to show a Princess Leia mask.

"I tried to find a pulse," Lucas said. "There isn't one. But she's still warm."

"Lucas . . ."

He wasn't trying to trick her, she knew that. Lucas had a sense of humor and his caper throwing eggs at the mayor's house proved that he didn't have the best sense of boundaries. He was genuinely bothered by what he'd found.

Kelly hoped that this was merely a prank that he'd fallen for. Gingerly, she reached into the garbage bag and let out a scream when she touched a body part that was definitely not made out of newspaper.

"Lucas," she whispered, "we have to get the police."

Even if they were wrong, Kelly thought. Even if, somehow, this was a joke, she and Lucas couldn't go any further in trying to figure it out. It was better to risk the derision of a policeman than to take a chance on meddling with a crime scene.

She stood up. Lucas followed her example. "I'll call 9-1-1," Kelly said.

"No one will be at the station," he said. "They're all out patrolling to keep an eye on the trick-or-treaters."

He was right. A call to the 9-1-1 dispatcher with the minimal information at hand was not going to send a squad car rushing to Daffodil Alley. If she sent Lucas to the police station to wait, it could take several hours before anyone responded.

"I suppose our best bet is to start walking and flag down an officer when we see a police car," she said.

"I know. It doesn't feel right to leave her like this," he said awkwardly, uncomfortable with feelings that had too many nuances for a teenage boy to understand.

Kelly patted him on the arm. "I know. But neither one of us is going to want to stay here."

Lucas swallowed. "I can stay if you want me too," he offered.

She could have hugged him for the kindness that prompted the offer, knowing that he felt badly for the dead girl, whoever she was, because she was cast aside in an alley, in a garbage bag. "No," Kelly said. "I think we'll both go together to find an officer. She's

—no one is likely to disturb her." She was past disturbing, whoever she was, Kelly thought.

4

OFFICER KENNEDY ARRIVES

Lucas bent back down and once again, fastened the drawstrings so that the bag was closed. As they made their way down the alley, he told her about being in the alley when he heard a car turn in.

"Something dropped," he said. "I didn't know what it was. Then the car drove down the alley, this way. I hid in the corner of the lot so no one would see me. Then I went down and I—I found her. I didn't know what it was," he said again.

'Maybe it's . . . maybe there's an explanation," Kelly said, trying to comfort him and knowing that, unless they were wildly off base, there was no explanation that could account for a body in a garbage bag. Why was she wearing a Princess Leia mask? What grotesque Halloween event could have led to such a horrible end?

They emerged from the alley onto Roosevelt Avenue. The sidewalks, still crowded, suddenly no longer seemed cheerful and benign to Kelly. Masks hid faces and in the darkness of the night, there was no assurance that here, among these parents and children and people celebrating the Halloween holiday, there wasn't someone who had committed a terrible deed.

"There!" Lucas pointed. "A police car just turned onto the street."

Inside the squad car, Troy Kennedy was traveling at something just above zero miles per hour, watching carefully to avoid hitting an overzealous child who might dart across the street in search of the next house where a light indicated that trick-or-treaters were welcome. The rain that threatened seemed to be holding off, so at least he didn't need his windshield wipers. It was seven-thirty. One more hour, and then trick-or-treating was over and the streets would be empty again and he could—

Troy hit his brakes and swore. Right in front of him, right in the middle of the street, a grown woman had stepped in front of the squad car. She had on enormous glasses, her hair was knotted up in a bun, and she was dressed like an old lady. He rolled down the window.

"Hey!" he shouted. "Be careful! There's a crosswalk, you know."

Undaunted, the woman approached the car. There was a young boy at her side, kind of scrawny looking, a Darth Vader mask on top of his head.

"Officer, we need your help," the woman said. Seen up close, Troy realized that she was dressed as an old woman, but she was actually young; the gray hair, a wig. "There's a body in a garbage bag at the end of Daffodil Alley."

"What kind of joke is this?" he demanded impatiently. It was bad enough when kids thought it would be funny to send the police on a wild goose chase, but adults ought to know better.

"It's not a joke," she said. "I'm Kelly Armello; I'm the librarian. I'm not in the habit of making up stories. Will you come?"

Troy sighed. "Lady, I'm supposed to be looking after the trick-or-treaters."

"There's a dead body in the alley," she retorted. "Are you going to do something about it or not?"

Of course, he was going to do something about it, Troy thought. He was going to cite her as soon as he checked out her crazy story. Blocking a police car was just the start of the charges he'd cite her for.

The officer pulled the car over to the side of the street. "Get in the back seat," he said. He doubted that either one of them was a threat, but he wasn't going to take a chance on some kind of mischief taking place that would leave him looking like a fool.

"Which end of Daffodil Alley?" he asked.

"The other end," Lucas spoke up.

"Not the Roosevelt Avenue end," Kelly clarified.

Troy didn't put on his lights or the siren. If this was a prank, he wasn't going to make a complete jackass of himself. For all he knew, there was a gang of people waiting in the alley ready to take a photo that would be posted on Facebook.

He turned into the alley at the librarian's direction.

"Here," Lucas said. "Be careful—she's in the corner. If you park here, you won't—you won't hit her."

Troy got out of the car, flashlight in hand, and let the librarian and Lucas out of the back seat. Lucas led the way.

"It's—she's there," he pointed. Troy followed Lucas's finger with his flashlight and saw the garbage bag, far enough away from the edge of the alley so that it wouldn't be in the way of any car driving through, but not near the trash cans at the corner of each back lot.

Troy had questions to ask if it was indeed a body, but he'd wait until he found out for sure. He bent down and pressed his hands against the outline of the contents within the bag.

"Is this where you found it?" he asked.

"No, she was in the street. I pulled her here so she wouldn't get hit by a car."

Lucas inched closer. "Whoever dropped her in the alley just left her there."

His indignation sounded genuine to Troy. He opened the garbage bag with deft, economical movements. His flashlight revealed a face hidden by a Princess Leia mask.

For an instant, Troy felt a rise of temper as he looked over his shoulder at Lucas, with a Darth Vader mask atop his head.

"She doesn't have a pulse," Lucas said.

Troy turned his attention back to the garbage bag and placed his fingers against her neck. Nothing.

He lifted the mask with one hand, using his other to hold the flashlight. He saw a young girl with bruises on her neck. There was the other evidence as well, but it would be up to the coroner to confirm those indications and give them a name. Troy left the girl where she was.

"Get back in the car," he told Kelly and Lucas, opening the door. "I'm radioing for help."

"Do we have to stay?" Lucas wanted to know.

"You're witnesses. You're the one who found the body," Troy said. "Yes, you have to stay."

Lucas was shivering, not only because the wind had shifted with the drop in temperature, and the rain that had threatened all evening had begun to fall, at first just a drop or two, but then more.

Troy swore and pulled the garbage bag up so that the body inside was completely covered. "Get in the car," he ordered.

Kelly was relieved to do as he ordered, Lucas less so. His chances of getting home before his mother were diminishing rapidly. And yet, fearful as he was of her reaction when she knew that he had disobeyed her orders to stay home, he wanted to be home, inside, with the lights on, the television on, the twins making noise, Marissa doing her homework at the kitchen table and telling him to turn the TV down because she was trying to study, Carrie and Mom talking about stuff that was boring. He'd rather be home, grounded, than out here in this dark alley, just a few feet away from a dead body in a garbage bag.

They heard Officer Kennedy giving terse instructions over the radio. It seemed like the person on the other end had a lot of questions. Lucas shivered. It was like on TV, sort of, but the person was real. She had been dressed like Princess Leia for Halloween and now she was dead.

"The ambulance will be coming," Officer Kennedy said. "After it gets here, I'll need to take you two to the station."

"Lucas will need to call his mother," Kelly said.

Troy nodded. "Where is she?"

"She's working," Lucas said. His teeth were chattering. Troy took off his jacket and handed it to Lucas, who stared at it as if he didn't know what to do with it. Kelly spread it over him so that it covered him. Troy got into the car and shut the door, then turned the heat up higher.

"Where does she work?"

"The Corner Café, but she doesn't get off until 9:30," Lucas said.

"It's ten o'clock," Troy told him.

Lucas stared. How could it possibly be so late? It had just been a short time ago that he'd entered the alley to wait for Chris and Tyler.

"I'll call her, Lucas," Kelly said, knowing that Lucas was frightened and uncertain and unsure of what to do next. She had Mrs. Krymanski's number in her contacts; the two had communicated often enough over Lucas's community service schedule.

Mrs. Krymanski answered right away. She always sounded as if she were angry. "Yes? Is he still at the library?"

"Mrs. Krymanski, no, he's—we're—there's been an —" suddenly Kelly was speechless.

"Lucas? Is he hurt?"

"No, no, he's not. He—can you come to the police station? We're going there now."

"The police station? What did he do? I told him not to leave the house tonight and he disobeyed me. He's grounded for the rest of the month!" Then, realizing that the month was over, Mrs. Krymanski amended her sentence. "He's grounded for the rest of the year. And Christmas break, too!"

"Mrs. Krymanski, Lucas was—someone has been killed, Lucas found the body."

Silence. "Is he all right?" Mrs. Krymanski asked, her voice stripped of its aggression as she tried to process the bewildering array of facts.

"Yes, he's . . . we're on our way to the police station. He found the body," Kelly repeated. "The police need to question him. We're waiting for the ambulance to come for the—for the body. Then we'll go to the police station."

"I'll be there right away."

Mrs. Krymanski ended the call.

"She's mad," Lucas said, resigned to his fate.

"Mad and scared and worried about you," Kelly said.

Troy had been able to hear Mrs. Krymanski's voice over the phone. She hadn't bothered trying to soften her tone. He remembered what Kyle had said earlier that day. *And the Krymanskis break the laws.* This kid didn't look like someone who would commit murder, and his mother didn't sound like the kind of woman who would tolerate misbehavior in her family. But there was a dead body in the alley and a Krymanski in the police car and from what Troy had learned since joining the police force, that match-up didn't bode well.

5

THE END OF A LONG DAY

elly's tone was businesslike when she called Carmela at home to explain why Lucas had asked her to leave the library to go with him. Carmela was a voracious gossip but if she found out the news about the dead girl from someone else, she'd be in a sulk for the rest of the week.

"I don't know," she answered. "I don't have any answers. I suppose the police will be investigating. I just wanted you to know."

"Will the library be closed tomorrow?"

"Closed? No, we'll open as usual." *Why would the library be closed*? Kelly wondered as she ended the call.

She needed to take a shower. She wanted to go to sleep. She wished the evening had not happened. She thought of poor Lucas, just a kid and not a bad kid, despite his family name and his youthful folly, answering the questions that had been put to him. Egging the mayor's house was a far cry from murdering a girl; would the authorities recognize that, or would they see this as a matter of delinquency's domino effect?

The state police had been called in; the police chief had made that decision quickly. Settler Springs didn't have the resources or experience to handle a murder. She hadn't gotten the impression that anyone on the local force wanted to handle it, either. The state police seemed to get called in for a lot of things. The police chief and the state policeman seemed to know each other pretty well. She wondered if they were related. The family ties of law enforcement in the area were well known. Maybe that was the reason why the state police were so obliging about helping out the Settler Springs Police Department.

She had been able to tell from the taut line of his jaw that Officer Kennedy felt that their own police department ought to have been given the authority to handle a murder in their own town, but he was a newcomer to the force. A newcomer to the town, too, she knew. She knew all the police officers; one of her annual children's programs was to take the preschoolers down to the station, where they were introduced to the officers, who told them how to be safe, not to talk to strangers and not to get into cars driven by people they didn't know, not to use drugs, and to let an officer know if anyone tried to hurt them. Then she would read "Officer Buckle and Gloria" to the kids. The officers would then hand out treats and drive them back to the library in the police cars.

Officer Kennedy hadn't been at the station when she'd taken the kids there in September; he wasn't on duty then, she supposed.

He hadn't been very friendly, but finding a dead body wasn't the sort of circumstance that would bring out the Officer Buckle in him, she thought wryly. She made a cup of coffee; there was no sense in worrying about caffeine tonight; she wasn't likely to sleep easily anyway.

Her thoughts kept returning to Lucas, answering their questions while his mother hovered over him as if she could protect her Krymanski son from danger. No one could seriously think that Lucas killed the girl, though, Kelly thought. He had found the body. He had sought Kelly because he didn't know what to do. He wasn't a murderer.

The police surely couldn't blame him. They couldn't!

Mrs. Krymanski would have a hard time affording a lawyer, if they charged Lucas. But they couldn't charge him. He hadn't killed the girl, whoever she was.

Kelly brightened. They'd have to identify her. That would reveal the killer. It was probably a boyfriend. Lucas didn't have a girlfriend. He didn't seem to want one yet. He was a young fourteen, with puberty barely manifesting itself yet. He liked to be with his friends and play basketball and video games. He was an indifferent student but not a troublemaker. He was just a kid who didn't have the advantages of coming from a family like the Truverts or the Starks, but that didn't make him a murderer. Mrs. Krymanski worked hard, and she was a single mom, but that didn't make her a lax parent. Quite the contrary. She wasn't the kind of mother who would cover up for her children if they misbehaved and she wasn't a parent who made unrealistic demands upon teachers when it came to her children's grades.

Lucas wasn't going to be applying for Harvard. He probably wasn't even going to apply to community college. College wasn't for everyone, if you needed someone to fix your leaky roof, you didn't ask if he had a PhD in philosophy. Lucas intended to go to the vo-tech school next year. He thought he'd take up welding, maybe, or auto mechanics. He wasn't quite sure, but he knew his abilities and his limitations and learning a trade was a smart option for a kid who would rather do physical work than study for a test. Just because he wasn't going to be in the running for class valedictorian didn't make him a murderer.

Kelly continued to present a series of arguments in her head for all the reasons why Lucas wasn't a murderer and hadn't killed the girl in the alley. But even after she'd dragged herself upstairs to take a shower and gone to bed, she couldn't rid herself of the suspicion that, to the police force, Lucas was the main suspect because he was a Krymanski.

She hadn't gotten that feeling from Officer Kennedy. His face was too hard to read. But she knew what Police Chief Roger Stark was thinking as he listened to Lucas re-tell the account of what had happened in the alleyway. And when the state police came, and Lucas had to tell his story again, their faces bore the same expression as that of the police chief. They knew all about the Krymanskis.

Everyone knew about the Krymanskis. But that didn't mean that it added up to murder. Besides, the Krymanskis ran more toward petty crime. Some drugs, that was true, among another branch of the family. But not murder. And why should it matter what the family was? Lucas was his own person. And he wasn't a murderer.

Troy Kennedy was thinking much the same thing when he went home after finishing his late shift. He'd gotten a text from Leo, who'd sent a photo of his grandchildren in their costumes, their trick-or-treat bags filled with Halloween loot. Troy smiled as he texted back to Leo to leave some candy for the kids. That photo was the only good thing that had happened on Halloween, he thought as he unlocked the front door of the house he rented and entered.

Arlo, the German Shepherd he'd rescued from the shelter just days before the dog was scheduled to be put down, greeted him with rapturous delight, making Troy's weariness fade just a bit as he put Arlo on the chain and let him outside.

As he filled Arlo's bowl with food, Troy thought again about the kid, Lucas. He didn't look like a killer. Troy didn't think he was a killer. Someone killed that girl, but Troy would bet it wasn't the Krymanski kid. Would the state police and the police chief bother to look for a suspect? They had let Mrs. Krymanski take her son home, but with a warning that they'd be asking more questions and he was to stick around.

Mrs. Krymanski had said that Lucas wouldn't be going anywhere but school and she'd fixed a fiery glare on her son. But Troy could tell that, behind the glare, Mrs. Krymanski was afraid.

Troy didn't blame her.

"C'mon in, Arlo, it's late," he said to the dog who obediently trotted back into the house and made for his food bowl.

Troy went into the living room and sat down on the couch, deciding against turning on the television because he knew that, by tomorrow, there would be news crews reporting in front of the police station and at the entrance to the alley. They'd be clamoring to find out the identity of the murdered girl and they'd want to know about the boy who'd found her. Lucas was a minor so his name wouldn't be revealed.

Unless the state police decided that he was the murderer and then the district attorney decided that Lucas would be tried as an adult. The DA wasn't a Stark or a Truvert, though, so he might not lean that way, Troy thought cynically.

Troy leaned back against the couch. He'd take Arlo out one more time before calling it a night. He'd set the coffee maker for the morning. He'd find out in the morning what there was to know about the murdered girl. She was young, it looked like, young enough to have parents who would notice if she didn't come home. But not as young as Lucas.

He couldn't get the kid out of his mind. He couldn't tell him to ditch the Darth Vader mask, but he had told him, before they went into the station, to take it off his head. Just carry it. Don't walk in wearing it. He could tell, by the quick side glance from the librarian, that she understood his reasoning, but he knew that if she'd had a chance, she'd have hidden the boy's mask. Just because Lucas was wearing a Darth Vader mask and the murdered girl had a Princess Leia mask, it wasn't proof that there was a connection.

All the same, he knew that as soon as Chief Stark found out about the Darth Vader mask, Lucas Krymanski was going to be his chief suspect in the murder of the girl in the Princess Leia costume.

6

MEETING ON THE TRAIL

During his military service, Troy had seen some things that would haunt him the rest of his life. Things that he had to come to terms with. Things that couldn't be neatly classified as right or wrong because they happened in a war zone, where life didn't come with guarantees and death was random and impersonal. He'd learned to deal with those things, and he thought he was handling civilian life pretty well.

But he'd been present when the police went to Mrs. Krymanski's house and took Lucas from her, and somehow, that image was just as powerful as the memories from Afghanistan. Lucas was just a frightened, skinny kid who looked scared to death, and his mother, all her bravado drained from her, had begged them to leave Lucas with her. She'd watch him, she'd make sure that he didn't go anywhere, he would listen to her.

Except he hadn't listened to her on Halloween night. He'd gone out for one of those kid flings and now he was a suspect in a murder.

The girl had been identified. She was a high school senior from Golden Ridge, a wealthy school district an hour away from Settler Springs. Her name was Tyra Cardew. Her father was a financial advisor in the city; her mother was a human resources manager for one of the region's banks. Tyra Cardew had an academic scholarship to Duquesne University, where she planned to study pre-med after graduation. She was an honor student, a cheerleader, and homecoming queen. And she had been two months pregnant when she died.

Troy Kennedy woke up early Sunday morning before the sun came up. He'd had a long, hard week, one in which sleep had been hard to come by. It was his day off and he had a list of things he needed to do around the house. Rake leaves. Take out the screens before the weather turned cold. Wash the car. Laundry.

But he needed to clear his head first. A week spent at the police station, where the guilt of a fourteen-year old kid was taken for granted because of his last name, while Police Chief Stark and Mayor Truvert didn't even bother to pretend that there was any reason to pursue any other suspect, had troubled him.

Troy got out of bed, threw the bedcovers back over the mattress, washed his face and brushed his teeth, pulled on sweats, and headed out the door. The night still ruled the sky but there was a hint of daylight breaking above. It was supposed to be a nice day. He drove out to the Trail, the scenic park the three boroughs maintained, for his daily run.

By the time he got there, daylight had dawned, and the sky looked like it might comply with the forecast that the meteorologist had given during last night's news. The news crews had been visible in Settler Springs for the entire week, broadcasting from the town's landmarks as they updated their audience on the latest details of the murder investigation. But now that Lucas had been taken into custody to a juvenile detention center, the news vans had gone too, deprived of the raw meat of speculation and titillating detail.

There only one other car in the parking lot at the Trail, a Prius. Troy had seen it there before during his runs, but he'd never seen the occupant.

He was surprised that more people weren't out for an early run, but he was glad that he'd have privacy. He wanted to be alone and he wanted to run fast and hard so that he'd physically expend himself to the point where he wouldn't see the scared look on Lucas Krymanski's face as the state police put handcuffs on him and took him away.

He was halfway up the Trail when a lone figure passed him. She looked vaguely familiar, but her head was covered by the hood of her jacket, and she ran as if she didn't want to be bothered by anyone. No danger of that; Troy wasn't in the mood for company. The trouble with being a police officer in a small town was that everyone knew him, and he didn't know them.

It felt good to run until he was tired and his muscles were protesting at the pace. The Trail ran along the river and was framed by the bright hues of the autumn leaves. Another week or another storm and the leaves would be down, the branches bare, the landscape barren as autumn surrendered to the bleakness of November.

It would be a lousy Thanksgiving for the Krymanski family, Troy thought as he turned to head back down the Trail. He'd heard that there had been some trouble for the family since Lucas had been arrested.

Mrs. Krymanski's boss had stood by her and since she worked in the kitchen; she wasn't visible to the clientele. But the oldest girl, a senior, had gotten into a fight when someone referred to her brother as "Killer Krymanski" and Troy had been called to the school. He had talked the other student's parents out of pressing charges, and he'd driven the girl home, pretending that he didn't hear her sobbing.

He slowed down as he came to the end of the Trail, then stopped abruptly. The person who belonged to the only other car in the lot was leaning against her Prius, her gaze focused on the Trail. When she saw him coming into the parking lot, she stood up and walked up to him.

"Officer Kennedy, I'm Kelly Armello," she said. "We met . . ."

She didn't finish. She didn't need to. She wasn't dressed like an old lady anymore, and now, with her hood off, he saw that she had a thick mane of curly red hair. Her eyes were dark brown, fringed with thick black lashes. She was tall and slender. Pretty. Prettier than he'd expect a librarian to be, although to be fair, he didn't know many librarians.

"I remember."

"What's going to happen to Lucas?" she demanded.

"There will be a trial—"

"Lucas didn't kill that girl," Kelly interrupted. "I can't believe that you just figure that he must have done it."

"He found the body," Troy said, stung by the accusation that it was his fault that Lucas had been arrested. "That's what they're going by."

She caught the nuance in his response. Suddenly the tight, hostile mask that had been her expression eased. "You don't think he's guilty either," she said triumphantly, as if she'd unearthed some kind of clue.

He didn't think Lucas was guilty, but he wasn't going to be discussing the details of a murder investigation with a civilian.

That's what he thought. That's what he meant. But it didn't explain why he found himself accepting her invitation to get coffee at The Corner Café.

"Why here?" he asked when they'd both gotten out of their cars in front of the restaurant, which did a booming breakfast business. "I don't think Mrs. Krymanski is going to want to see me."

"She's not working today," Kelly answered. "She's going to visit Lucas."

They had to wait fifteen minutes before they were seated. Troy felt conspicuous to be standing there, conscious of the curious gazes of the other people who were noticing his presence. Or maybe, he thought, they were noticing Miss Armello. She was worth noticing.

A waitress that Kelly greeted by her first name showed them to a booth. Kelly moved so that she could sit facing the door. He supposed she wanted to notice who came in. Maybe it was bad for a librarian's reputation to be seen in the company of a cop.

She took off her hoodie. "I'm always starving after a run," she said. "Have you eaten here before?"

"Lunch, a couple of times." Leo liked to eat here, and Troy had been here with him when they worked the same shift. Troy didn't much care where he ate; he generally preferred to go home for lunch. A sandwich and a can of soup satisfied him, and he liked the solitude of his own home, with just Arlo at his feet, hoping against hope that a piece of the sandwich would fall to the floor.

"I can vouch for the omelets," she said, closing the menu. "It won't be as good as if Mrs. Krymanski was making it, but it'll be good."

He was surprised when she gave her order; he wouldn't have expected such a slender woman to be able to do justice to a menu item that described itself as the "Hungry Man's Breakfast." He was confident that he could dispatch pancakes, ham, home fries, and coffee without any problem but he didn't know where she'd put it all.

"Lucas didn't do it," she said as soon as the waitress had taken their order and left.

Troy sighed. "There's no other suspect,"

"No one has bothered to try to find one," she retorted. "What are you going to do about that?"

A PRIVATE INVESTIGATION

By the time they'd finished eating breakfast and she'd paid for the meal—she insisted, laughing, because she said she'd taken him hostage and it was the least she could do—Troy realized that all of his stereotypical ideas about librarians were wrong. Kelly Armello wasn't dowdy or prim; she had a rich laugh and a vibrant smile. She could eat as much as a trucker and the waitress refilled her coffee cup three times.

She was also stubborn, persistent, and didn't intend to take no for an answer. "There's nothing I can do about it," he protested when they left the restaurant. "The investigation is over."

"What investigation? There wasn't one. They want an easy case and so they arrested Lucas. Can you honestly see a girl like that being involved with Lucas? He's just a kid."

"That doesn't mean he doesn't notice girls."

"Of course, he notices them," Kelly said impatiently. "But he doesn't actually engage with them romantically."

"What about the Princess Leia mask?"

"Do you know how many kids dressed as Star Wars characters for Halloween?" she rebutted. "Star Wars costumes are the second most popular choice for Halloween. Harry Potter is first."

That sounded like the kind of thing a librarian would know.

"You have to admit; it didn't look good for Lucas when he showed up with that mask."

"He should have left it in the police car," she said.

He didn't bother to tell her that at that stage of the investigation, concealing the fact that Lucas had been wearing a Darth Vader mask would only have made the boy look even guiltier.

"That's not how to prove his innocence."

"Then you tell me how to prove it, Officer Kennedy, because that boy is not a killer, and I intend to do whatever I can to prove his innocence. And I'm counting on you to help me."

"Me? Why me?"

"Because I don't think you want to see an innocent kid blamed for a murder he didn't do."

"No, I don't," he said angrily. "But I can't start up an investigation that's been closed!"

Their raised voices were attracting attention from passers-by heading into the restaurant.

"Look, I have things to do," Troy said.

"Nothing you have to do is as important as finding the person who killed that girl," Kelly said. "Go home, do what you have to do. I'll meet you at the library at six o'clock."

"The library?"

"It'll be closed. We'll be able to go over what we know and try to figure out what we need to do."

"We don't need a library to do that. I owe you dinner."

She grinned; she had a cute dimple in the corner of her cheek that curved when she smiled. "That's right, you do. Where do you want to meet? Settler Springs doesn't have a lot of restaurants."

"I was thinking of my place." He wasn't sure why he was inviting her to his home. But he didn't retract the invitation.

She raised her eyebrows. "Are you a good cook?" she asked. There was a no-nonsense, straightforward expression in her eyes that told him that an invitation to his house had better mean dinner and nothing more.

"No, but I'm great at picking up take-out. Chinese, pizza, you name your preference, and I'll have it on the table. And I'll even use real plates."

She studied him for a few moments as if she were making up her mind. Troy stood up under her scrutiny. He wasn't planning to attack her. He just didn't like eating out all that much and he placed a lot of faith in Arlo's assessment of character. If Arlo didn't like her, well, that would tell him all he needed to know.

"Okay," she said. "Where do you live?"

"I'll pick you up," he said.

"Not yet," she told him with a smile that eased the refusal. "I'll come over. It'll be okay. I'm a librarian. Your neighbors will assume I'm teaching you how to read."

"My neighbors," Troy said drily, "will be happy to see someone besides my dog, Arlo, coming into the house. They don't approve of my lack of a social life."

"Where do you live?"

"On Jefferson, 512 Jefferson."

She nodded. "You must be the only person on Jefferson who's under thirty years old."

"I'm thirty-two," he said.

"Close enough. I'll be there at six. I'm always on time, so if I knock on the door and you're not there, I'll take it as a sign that you changed your mind."

"I'm never late and the food will be on the table. Pizza or Chinese?"

"General Tso's, fried rice, shrimp egg roll, wonton soup."

The doorbell rang promptly at six, setting off Arlo's barking response. Troy glanced around the rooms for a quick inspection. He'd cleaned, dusted, and vacuumed so that every room she would see was neat. She wasn't going to see his bedroom, so it didn't matter that his clothes were heaped on the bureau and his shoes were piled in the corner.

The leaves outside hadn't been raked, but the bathroom inside was pristine. The car hadn't gotten washed, but the furniture smelled of lemon polish. Plates, silverware and glasses were on the table, waiting for pepperoni pizza and General Tso's chicken and wine to be served.

"Hi," he greeted.

"Hi," she said. "I brought dessert," she handed him a bakery box.

Arlo went to greet her. She responded by kneeling down and rubbing his fur. "Hey, baby," she said. "You must be Arlo."

Arlo bumped his nose against her knee.

"It's a sign of affection," Troy said. "He has a strange way of showing that he likes you."

"Learned behavior?" she asked, giving Troy a quizzical glance.

She made him laugh. She wasn't flirtatious at all, he realized. She just said what she thought. He liked it. He wasn't exactly sure what to do, but even the novelty had its appeal because it was obvious from the get-go that Kelly Armello wasn't the kind of woman who would pretend to be something she wasn't. Kelly didn't have an image to project; she was exactly what she seemed to be. He realized that most of the women he'd known in the past started out with an image that was a composite of what they wanted to appear to be and what they thought he wanted a woman to be. The real woman underneath took time to find and by that time, sometimes it hadn't really been worth the emotional excavation that was involved. That wasn't Kelly. He didn't know much about her, but he knew she was real.

She was wearing blue jeans and a green sweater and boots. It sounded more mundane in words than it looked on her. She was curvier than her slenderness had indicated and her hair, loose now, made a vivid red cloud of curls around her heart-shaped face.

He was glad that he'd shaved before she arrived. He doubted that he looked as good in jeans and a flannel shirt as she looked in her attire, but maybe shaving helped.

Kelly didn't hide the fact that as she went with him into the kitchen, she was noticing the look of the rooms.

"Does it pass inspection?" he asked when they were both seated at the table.

"You're a better housekeeper than I am," she admitted.

"Company is a great inspiration for a dust cloth," he said.

"So, you're not a neat freak," she said. "That's good. I figure that if dust was good enough for God to use to make a man, who am I to sweep it up and throw it away?"

"Are you planning to build a roommate out of your dust?"

She grinned. "No, but I have enough of it to do that if I wanted to."

"So," he said when their plates were occupied by the foods they'd chosen and their wineglasses were filled, "where do you want to start?"

"Start with what you know." She took a small notebook and a pen out of her purse, waiting, fork in one hand, pen in the other, for him to proceed.

"I know what you know," he said.

"Okay, then what do the police know?"

"What the police 'know' is an overstatement. They know that Lucas Krymanski found a body in Daffodil Alley on Halloween night at some point after six-thirty. They know who the murdered girl is."

"Well?" she asked when he stopped talking.

"You asked what they know. That's what's known. From that point, they decided that Lucas killed her."

"You don't agree."

"You already know that I don't agree. But no one asked. The state police arrested Lucas for the murder."

"Do they think he got her pregnant?"

"They haven't made that point yet."

"Yet?"

"I don't know if they're going to pursue it."

"Wouldn't the assumption be that her boyfriend got her pregnant and killed her because of it?"

"That's an assumption. They don't know her boyfriend."

"They aren't investigating?"

"I told you, the case is closed and awaiting trial as far as the police are concerned."

"Then it's up to us," she said, putting down her pen. She raised her wine glass. "To justice."

He raised his own glass but didn't clink it against hers. "Justice might be too ambitious," he said darkly. "Let's just toast to proving that Lucas didn't kill her."

Kelly nodded. Their glasses touched. "Is this where we spit on our hands and make a pact never to trust anyone but ourselves and to reveal nothing until we've uncovered the truth?" she asked.

"I don't think I've ever shared a meal with a woman who made an offer like that," he said. "Is this a date?

She smiled. "Not yet," she said.

"Is it me or baggage from someone else?"

Kelly shook her head. "I'm single. My boyfriend and I have been apart for six months. We're 'still friends,'" she said, grimacing at the term. "What about you?"

"Single. My fiancée and I broke up when I went to Afghanistan for the second time. I guess we're still friends, although since she married one of my friends, I wouldn't swear to it." Troy shrugged. "It was another life in another time."

"You don't want her back?"

"I don't want her back."

"What was her name?"

"Angela. Why?"

"All stories have characters," she said whimsically. "And all characters have names."

"Okay, I don't know what that means."

"It means that, even though this isn't a date, I don't think we need to invite Angela to the table."

8

LIBRARY SLEUTHING

He was good looking. Very good looking. Dark hair, dark eyes, tall, lean. No annoying mannerisms. A sense of humor. He wore the Settler Springs male uniform of jeans and a flannel shirt with ease.

She liked his dog. Arlo was well-behaved and affectionate. That was a good sign. You could tell a lot about a person from their pets; Kelly was convinced of that. She was still mourning the loss of her cat Jade, who had died the winter before. Jade had been the family cat for eighteen years, a tenure that had given her rank in the household, where she was petted and adored and treated like the royalty she had believed herself to be. What would Jade have thought of Arlo, Kelly wondered. And what would she have thought of Officer Kennedy?

She hadn't intended to pursue Officer Kennedy romantically when she saw him on the Trail. Noticing that a man was nice-looking was a function of eyesight. Appreciating his sense of humor was not an invitation. She could not deny that she had been aware of him in a manner which invited contemplation on the subject. But her intentions had been entirely focused upon Lucas and they still were. Finding out that Troy believed he was innocent as well galvanized her; together, they could prove that Lucas was not a killer.

Not that she needed to be galvanized. Troy's cautious approach was completely opposite her own response to a situation. Some of it was, she supposed, the result of his military background. Don't rush in until every possible danger had been assessed. Some of it, she suspected, might be a tendency toward cynicism. Maybe that was Angela's fault, Kelly thought. Losing a fiancée to a friend had to sting.

Some of it might be due to his being the newest officer on the force; he had been there long enough to sense that the family ties in Settler Springs were, in some ways, more powerful than the laws that the police department was sworn to uphold. It was interesting that when he referred to the police, he said 'they', not 'we' as if he felt distance from his fellow officers. Was it the newness of the employment or was it distrust?

And did it matter, she asked herself as she finished the monthly statistical report? He wasn't going to hide from the truth, and he believed that Lucas was innocent.

"Good morning," she said to Carmela, who arrived, as always, five minutes late with the usual story about traffic at the stop light. There was never traffic in Settler Springs, but five minutes wasn't a hardship as long as the doors opened promptly at ten o'clock in the morning.

Carmela, who had enjoyed the notoriety of being in a town with a murder case, missed the excitement of the news vans parking in front of the library. "Do you think they've found out anything new?" she asked as she picked up books to re-shelve.

"I haven't heard anything," she said.

"Officer Kennedy didn't have any news?"

"Officer Kennedy?"

"I heard you two had breakfast yesterday morning at The Café."

She should have known. "We were both running on the Trail," Kelly explained. "We got breakfast. If he knows anything about the case, he didn't tell me." That wasn't a lie. He didn't know anything because the case wasn't being investigated the way it should be. But she knew she needed to protect Troy from gossip. He was the new guy on the force, and he wasn't part of the code of silence.

Disappointed, Carmela left the circulation desk to put books away. But her speculation soured Kelly's mood. No one seemed to care whether an injustice was being committed and no one thought about what being locked up could do to a fourteen-year-old boy who wasn't a street kid. She needed to go somewhere and do something beyond Carmela's pervasive aura of peevishness.

"Who's on the homebound delivery list?" she asked when Carmela returned to the circulation desk.

The library had gotten a grant to deliver books to homebound patrons. It was Carmela's job to deliver the books and while she enjoyed doing it when the homebound patrons were people from her church or were known to her, she didn't like everyone.

"Mrs. Hammond, and I don't know why she's on the list. She should move to the high-rise where she wouldn't have to climb the stairs. The only reason she doesn't is because if she lived in the high-rise, she wouldn't be able to look out her window and see everything that's going on in Daffodil Alley and—"

"Do you want me to deliver her books?" Kelly interrupted. Daffodil Alley! Maybe Mrs. Hammond had seen something.

"She'll talk your ear off," Carmela warned, happy to surrender the task but feeling obligated to alert Kelly to the perils that went with it. "You won't get out of there in less than forty-five minutes."

Kelly was already on her feet and had her coat on. "That's okay. I'll stop at the bank first and make the deposit, then I'll deliver Mrs. Hammond's books."

She put the satchel with the books in her car, went to the bank, and then drove to Lincoln Avenue and parked her car in front of the building where Mrs. Hammond lived on the second floor above the jewelry shop. She rang the doorbell and waited, knowing that it would take the older lady a little while to come down the stairs.

When she opened the door, Mrs. Hammond was beaming happily. "Oh, Kelly, it's so good to see you," she said. "You go first, dear, you'll be much faster than me."

Mrs. Hammond had a tray on the coffee table in front of her living room sofa. "Let me take your coat, dear," she said. "Is it getting cold out?"

"It's not too bad, but it's November, and we know what that means."

"I have tea to warm you up. Now you sit down and show me what you've brought me."

Mrs. Hammond was a fan of many genres and when choosing her books, Kelly made sure that she brought a variety. Mrs. Hammond nodded with pleasure as Kelly showed her the books."

"Oh, that's a lovely assortment," she said. "I've put the books to be returned by the stairs for you to take when you leave. But I hope you can stay for a bit?"

"I'm happy to do that," Kelly said, accepting the cup of tea.

Kelly and Mrs. Hammond chatted about the books they were reading. Mrs. Hammond's memory of literature extended back for decades. She remembered when *The Catcher in the Rye* was considered a disreputable book, and she could chuckle over the scandal that accompanied the publication of *Peyton Place*.

"People make such a fuss over what they think is obscene," Mrs. Hammond said. "But no one is forcing them to read it."

"No. Well, I suppose people are easily bothered by things they regard as bad behavior. I imagine that you see quite a few things up here, from your vantage point, that go on below."

"I do indeed," Mrs. Hammond agreed. "Couples are much more open these days. I believe they call it PDAs?"

Kelly grinned. "You see a lot of public displays of affection?" she asked, amused that the old lady was familiar with the jargon.

"Much more so than when I was a girl. We'd never have kissed a boy out in the street. But I suppose times change." Then Mrs. Hammond's face grew stern. "But that's not what bothers me. It's the drugs. I see them, right out there, bold as brass. I see people coming to get them."

"On Lincoln Avenue?" Kelly asked, feigning surprise. Lincoln Avenue, while not as busy as Roosevelt Avenue, was a public street and not at all the location where drug transactions were likely to take place.

"Oh, no, not out front. There, over in the alley," Mrs. Hammond said, pointing to the side window which looked out upon Daffodil Alley. "I still have my lighted pumpkin up," she apologized. "I'll be putting my turkey up soon."

"You see drug sales in the alley?" Kelly asked, steering Mrs. Hammond back to the subject of crime.

"I used to go to the council meetings every month when I could walk better. I told them what was going on. But they never paid any attention. They told me they'd send an officer, but they never did. Now, I can't go to the meetings any more, but I still see what goes on."

"Have you seen anything recently?"

Mrs. Hammond paused. "I saw a car, the night of the murder," she said. "It's the car I always see."

Kelly hid her excitement. Here, finally, was a clue that Troy would be willing to regard as significant.

"A car?"

"Yes, that sporty little red car."

"Did anyone ask you what you saw that night?"

"You mean the police?" Mrs. Hammond asked scornfully. "They don't ask questions because they wouldn't like the answers."

"What do you mean?"

"You've lived here most of your life, Kelly, except when you went away to college. You know what I mean. Have a cookie. I baked them this morning. I don't have the same touch I used to have, but they aren't too bad. I got the recipe from one of those baking mysteries. Those are a lot of fun to read."

Kelly brought Mrs. Hammond back to the topic of Settler Springs. "I've lived here since I was eight years old, when my dad took the job of school superintendent."

"Then you know. Or your dad did, I'm sure. Certain children got in trouble, but others didn't, even when they did the same things."

"He was bothered by the unfairness," Kelly revealed. "He said it happens in all school districts, but it seemed to be worse here. He took an early retirement, and now he and my mom travel a lot."

Mrs. Hammond nodded. "Good for them. And you still live in the house where they lived. I like that."

"It's still their address, even though they're almost never there. In the winter they go to Florida and during the rest of the year, they mostly travel. They stay here in the spring. But on Halloween night . . . you said you saw a car?"

"Not 'a' car, Kelly. The car I always see. The red car."

"Whose car is it?"

"It belongs to the young man who sells the drugs, of course. I see him in the alley. I look out; you'd be surprised how much light these holiday ornaments provide. I see him come into the alley, after dark, and then I see people coming and leaving quickly. No one is there long, except for him."

"Was he selling drugs on Halloween night?"

Mrs. Hammond shook her head. "He drove part way down the alley, just far enough not to be seen from Lincoln Avenue. He lifted something from the back seat. I didn't know what it was then, but it must have been the murdered girl. He put the bag on the ground and then he drove away. I didn't think anything of it at the time, since no one else came."

"You didn't call anyone?"

"My dear, they would just say I was a senile old lady who reads too many crime novels," Mrs. Hammond said realistically. "When Harry was alive and we lived on Monroe, I used to go to the council meetings to complain about the drugs. Then, when I first moved here after Harry died, I called about the drugs instead. No one came and no one wanted to know anything. Why would I call about anything now?"

9

TRYING TO SOLVE THE PERFECT
CRIME

"If she didn't get a license plate number," Troy pointed out, "it's going to be hard to make a connection between the driver of the car and the murdered girl."

"But it's something," Kelly insisted. "It's proof that Lucas wasn't lying about the car."

"We can let Lucas's lawyer know," Troy said. "Do you think she'd be willing to testify?"

"I don't think she's afraid," Kelly said. "But she's convinced that no one will believe her. She's old, she doesn't get around well, she's known for being someone who calls the borough office and the police station to complain. Still, she saw the car. A red, sporty car."

"That could be anything to a woman as old as she is. She might be thinking of a Stutz-Bearcat."

"Mrs. Hammond knows what PDAs are," Kelly retorted. "I think she knows a sports car from a Stutz-Bearcat."

They were in a sports bar. *Monday Night Football* was on every television and the noise of the diners made it easy for them to discuss the progress of their investigation. Ever since learning from Carmela that her shared breakfast with Troy had been seen and commented on, Kelly thought it better if they were discreet. Nothing could be allowed to prejudice their progress in proving Lucas's innocence. The sports bar was a half hour away from Settler Springs and unlikely to be patronized by town residents, who would be watching the game at home.

"The Stutz-Bearcat was a sports car," Troy replied.

"Circa 1911," came the response.

"Is there anything you don't know?"

"I don't know who killed Tyra Cardew, but I know it wasn't Lucas."

"Okay. So, we have a potential witness. Maybe there's something there. You know what bothers me?"

"Everything about this case."

"Besides that. The girl's father. Wouldn't you think he'd have some questions about who killed his daughter?"

"Maybe he believes Lucas is guilty."

"His daughter is from a wealthy family, top-notch. She's pretty and popular. Why would she be hanging out with a fourteen-year-old kid who lives almost an hour away?"

"No one asked him? Or the mother?"

"I told you, no one has asked anything." Troy didn't add that he hadn't brought the questions up, either. It was apparent that as far as the Settler Springs Police Department was concerned, the case was solved, the murderer found, and justice was done. He'd broached the subject with Leo and with Kyle, shortly after the murder happened, but neither had much information nor did either seem interested. The state police were handling it. Leo wasn't as down on the Krymanskis as Kyle was, but even he was conditioned to believe that crime was a Krymanski dominant trait.

"Can't you ask?" Kelly said eagerly. "You could find the address in the police report, couldn't you?"

It was the same idea that had been germinating in Troy's mind since the girl had been identified. "I don't have any reason to question them," he said. "The case is closed, remember."

"And the killer is still at large!" Kelly put down her fork. "It's worth asking the father if he has anything to add to the report."

"I could go by after class tomorrow," Troy said thoughtfully. "I'll be in the city anyway. I can call and ask if he'd rather meet at home or at his place of work."

"And after the library closes, I can go home by the alley," Kelly said. "Maybe I'll hang around and see what I see."

"No!"

Fortunately, Troy's loud objection wasn't overheard by the vocal diners at the sports bar; the New England Patriots quarterback had just been sacked and the Steeler fans were jubilant.

"What do you mean? Mrs. Hammond knows that something is going on in the alley. I don't think murder is going to stop drug traffic. Don't you want to find out about the car?"

"I don't want you going into an alley and taking a risk."

"I run really fast, you know. I'd be out of the alley before they could catch me."

"One dead body in the alley is enough," he said in a tone of voice that indicated he wasn't going to change his opinion. She was naïve if she thought that running fast was enough to elude criminals who were eluding notice. She was someone who acted before she thought, just like on Halloween night when she'd gotten his attention by standing right in front of his car. If he'd been going any faster, he could have hit her. But that hadn't occurred to her and she was just as likely to be impulsive if she were caught in the alley by anyone who didn't want to be seen.

"What should we do, then?"

The pronoun pleased him. What should 'we' do? It was nice to be on the inside of that 'we' even though they weren't actually a couple. They weren't actually anything, he realized. They weren't even friends, really. Just two people who didn't want Lucas Krymanski to go to prison for a crime they knew he hadn't committed.

"I'll drive by the alley," he said. "It won't seem strange, since there was a murder there."

"If you drive by in a police car, anyone who's there will scatter. I know! I'll ask Mrs. Hammond to give me a call if she notices anything going on in the alley."

Troy shook his head. "We don't want to get her involved in this. She's an old lady and she's vulnerable."

"Then you come up with an idea." But it wasn't in Kelly's nature to let someone else take charge of the creative thinking. "Why don't we do a stakeout?" she suggested, her eyes animated with the idea as it struck her.

He laughed. "You sound like a librarian who's been reading too many crime novels."

"Maybe I am," she answered, the dimple in her cheek doing a kind of hula dance as she grinned. "But that doesn't mean it's a bad idea."

"We'd have to have a good hiding place," he said, picking up on the notion, even though he'd made fun of it. "We'd need to be in a car so we'd be hidden, but we'd have to be able to see what's going on."

"All the stores have back lots," she pointed out.

"Not many cars, though. The business owners go home after they close. The lots don't have anything but trash cans."

"A lot of trash cans," she brightened. "They'd make a great hiding place. And it's dark back there; no one would see us."

He wasn't keen on the idea of giving up the relative security of a car. To be exposed in an alley that had turned into a spot which had its share of crime didn't inspire optimism. Not to mention that they'd be pretty uncomfortable, hiding on the cold cement on a chilly fall night.

"There isn't any other plan that will work," she persisted when he remained silent.

"Let me think about it," he said. "Something might come to me."

"Uh-huh. You'll decide not to do it."

He was stung by the implied criticism. "It's not a chapter in a book, you know. Turning the page won't make everything turn out right. If drugs are being sold there, you can be sure someone has a gun. A red car that's associated with drugs doesn't prove that the driver killed the girl, at least not in terms that will convince the law. Yes, it's suspicious," he said, holding up his hand to stave off her immediate protest. "But no one saw a license plate in the dark. And if we're going to be solving this, we're doing it unofficially, so we can't count on any support from the police. We'll need more than suspicions. The drug sellers, if they're also killers, won't need more than suspicion, though, if we're seen. They'll take care of the problem."

"You're a cop. You have a gun," Kelly pointed out as if he were slow in connecting the obvious dots, ignoring everything that he had just said.

"I'm not going to be in uniform." But her words brought up an interesting puzzle. He'd never heard a word about drug trafficking in Settler Springs from any of the officers on the force. If the old lady had called the borough office about what she'd seen, why hadn't the police investigated?

It was something to pursue. Maybe he'd ask Leo or Kyle. It was no use asking Chief Stark; he upheld the mayor's line that Settler Springs was a nice, quiet town with almost no crime except when the Krymanskis got into trouble. If he'd been told about Mrs. Hammond's calls, he probably had dismissed the information just as most people were dismissive of old people. But Troy knew, from living on Jefferson Avenue, that old people noticed everything. His neighbors knew when everyone on the street left in the morning and when they came home. They knew who had gotten packages from UPS and who had company coming. Even though Jefferson really was a tranquil neighborhood, the residents would know what parts of town had secrets they were hiding. Maybe he needed to start asking around, in a casual way, to find out more. A red car shouldn't be hard to pin down.

10

MEETING THE DEAD GIRL'S
PARENTS

He wasn't sure what kind of reception he'd get from the father of the murdered girl when he called, identified himself as a member of the Settler Springs Police Department, and asked if he could meet with him to go over a few things. The man immediately agreed to meet. His house, seven o'clock.

Troy's class had ended two hours before that, so he stopped to get something to eat before driving to Golden Ridge, a neighborhood which exuded an impression of sleek comfort. The homes were all architectural splendors, the landscaping was carefully and exquisitely maintained, and every car that wasn't in its garage was something well above the average person's pay scale.

The door opened as soon as he knocked.

"I'm Les Cardew," said the man at the door. He was a man in his late forties or so without a speck of gray in his hair, a physique which indicated that only regular trips to the gym were holding off middle-age spread, and a piercing gaze. "This is Lauren, my wife. It's taken you guys long enough to show up."

Mrs. Cardew's eyes were red; for the family of the murdered girl, the case wasn't closed and wouldn't be for a long time, regardless of who was convicted of the crime.

"May I come in?" Troy asked, puzzled by the man's comment.

Mr. Cardew opened the door wider. Mrs. Cardew led him into a room off to the side. All the furniture was white. The floors were gleaming hardwood. The Cardews, Troy decided, must not have pets. He could only imagine what his living room would look like if Arlo had free rein to a white couch.

There were trophies in a case by the window. "They were Tyra's. Softball," Mr. Cardew said, noticing that Troy's attention had been caught by the trophy case. "She got an academic scholarship to Duquesne, but she could just as easily have gotten an athletic scholarship for softball somewhere. She was good. They won the championship this year."

"Sit down, Officer," Mrs. Cardew said. "Can I get you anything?"

"No, thank you. I appreciate you seeing me."

"What took so long?" Mr. Cardew demanded. "We've been waiting for someone to ask us real questions."

"I'm sorry . . . real questions?"

"Officer, I don't want to come off like a snob. Our daughter was beautiful, accomplished, popular. She had a boyfriend, someone she'd met through a friend. A college student. We hadn't met him yet, but she said she would introduce us. She said he was busy with studies and didn't have the time to meet us until Christmas break. I wasn't happy about that, but . . ." he shrugged his shoulders in defeat. "Nothing I could do about it. When I saw the picture of this kid they'd pinned for the murder, I said to Lauren, 'there's no way that Tyra was involved with him.' He's—" Mr. Cardew struggled to find the words. "He's not her sort," he finished lamely.

"Can you fill me in on what you told the police?"

"It's in the report," Mr. Cardew said. "Not that the cop wrote much down. He said they'd found the murderer, this fourteen-year-old. Officer, I'm not saying my daughter was perfect. They told us that she was—pregnant. I'm not happy about that, but what difference does it make now? I don't know who the father is, but it wasn't some fourteen-year-old kid who looks like he doesn't shave yet."

"There were no signs of rape," Mrs. Cardew said quietly. "We asked the officer."

"There weren't any signs of sex, period," her husband said. "Whatever happened that night, it wasn't a—whatever they're trying to make it seem like, that wasn't it. Tyra has her own car. It was gone on Halloween night; she said she was going to a party. It was Halloween; we didn't think anything of it. She was going as Princess Leia. She told us that her boyfriend was going as Han Solo. Her car was found in the parking lot of a shopping plaza where she left it. She didn't drive to the party. Her boyfriend must have picked her up, or else friends did, and drove to the party. You can't tell me that a fourteen-year old kid drove out this way, picked her up, drove her back to that town, and killed her. What I want to know is why your police department is so sure that this Kermanski kid, whoever he is, killed my daughter. I'll bet you he never met her until that night, when he found her body—"

Mr. Cardew covered his face with his hands. Sobs came from his body as if they were escaping a long time of imprisonment. His wife put her arm around him, and the couple sat close, sharing their grief.

"I'm sorry," Mr. Cardew said, wiping his eyes with the back of his hand. "Tyra—she was our daughter. Your officers, the state police, the police captain, they made her sound like she was some kind of cheap . . . they said that we needed to protect her reputation or else what would come out in court would tarnish her memory. They said—"

Troy felt a surge of anger. How could anyone deny these people the right to have a resolution, if not to their grief, at least to the uncertainty?

"Mr. Cardew," Troy said. "You need to remember your daughter as you knew her. If you're willing to find out the truth, whatever it is, in order to find out what really happened to your daughter and why she was murdered, then that's what you need to do."

Mr. Cardew looked at Troy in disbelief. "What are you saying?"

"I don't have any kids," Troy said. "But if I did . . . I'd want to make sure they were treated right, in life and in death. If you're not satisfied with the investigation so far, then make some noise about it.

I'm guessing you could get some attention if you wanted to. Mrs. Krymanski can't afford a lawyer who can pursue her son's case so that all the answers come out. But money isn't going to stand in your way, is it?"

"Money doesn't mean anything. It won't bring Tyra back."

"Then don't let Tyra be lost," Troy urged.

His drive back to Settler Springs was haunted by the image of a girl he'd never met when she was alive. When he thought of her, it was with the Princess Leia's mask on her face and the bruises on her neck. He'd seen enough death in Afghanistan, but this was different. This girl wasn't in a war zone.

He didn't feel like going home, and that was unusual. Home was a sanctuary, and Arlo was all the welcoming committee he wanted. But as he drove past the library and saw that the lights were still on, he pulled his car into a parking space and went inside.

Kelly was helping a patron at the computer station when she saw him enter. Her eyes widened and he could practically see question marks in her pupils. Despite his disheartened mood, she made him smile. She didn't hide her feelings or her thoughts, and her face revealed everything. He paused by the magazine rack until she had finished assisting the patron, who put on headphones and paid no attention to anyone.

"You're alone here?"

"Carmela has choir practice."

"Is it safe for you to be here alone?"

She laughed. "It has been so far," she said. "Are you in here to rob the petty cash drawer?"

"Maybe next time. When do you close up?"

"Why? Did you learn anything from the Cardews?"

"Mr. Cardew doesn't understand why no one asked him real questions. He doesn't believe Lucas killed her or that he got her pregnant or drove all the way down to Golden Ridge—"

"Lucas doesn't have a driver's license or a car, he's fourteen!" Kelly interrupted.

"I know. That's what Mr. Cardew said, too. He doesn't know that the Krymanskis get blamed for everything in town. He just doesn't get why the local police, and the state police, don't care enough about finding the real killer."

"What did you tell him?'

"I told him to make a stink about it, more or less. He's someone people would listen to. If he thinks the crime is being swept under the rug, he can get attention. I think he'd rather be doing something besides grieving."

"I don't blame him," Kelly said somberly. "It has to be terrible to wake up, day after day, with his daughter's death the first thought in his head. And then to see blame being placed on a kid who's so obviously not the killer . . . you know what doesn't make sense?"

None of it made sense to Troy. "What?" he asked.

"Why don't the police want to find the killer? They have to know, deep down, that Lucas didn't do it. So that means that there's a killer loose. Why wouldn't they want that killer caught? What if he kills again?"

"If her boyfriend killed her because she was pregnant," Troy said logically, "there's no reason to worry about him killing again. He would have killed Tyra to get rid of a problem."

"But why would he come all the way out here from Golden Ridge to dump her body in an alley?"

"Because . . . because he's from Settler Springs," Troy reasoned, "and the alley is a place he knows."

11

NOT A CHAPTER IN A BOOK

Kelly's stake-out idea didn't seem so crazy anymore, not once Troy had the time to put all the puzzle pieces into place. It seemed obvious. No one really noticed alleys; they were forgotten streets that worked for short-cuts to get across town, but they weren't important. Someone who was dealing drugs would have a different perspective of Daffodil Alley. The alley was his office.

He knew there was no way of talking Kelly out of accompanying him to the alley. He tried, but she was having none of it. When he called her to tell her that he was going to start hanging around the alley to see if anything was going on now that the town was convinced the murder was solved and the killer awaiting trial, Kelly objected immediately.

"The library closes at 8:30," she said. "I can change before then—I'll tell Carmela I'm going running—and I'll meet you in Daffodil Alley within fifteen minutes."

"She's not going to believe you've developed a passion for exercise in the dark," he said. "The sidewalks in town are so uneven that you'd end up with a broken ankle."

"I'm not really going running," she said. "That's just an excuse."

"Remind me, the next time I'm trying to solve a murder, not to get tangled up with a librarian who reads too many mysteries."

Kelly laughed. "It's an occupational hazard."

Hazard was the right word, Troy thought grimly as they entered the alley through a circuitous network of back lots and yards so that they would not be seen entering from either the Roosevelt or the Lincoln ends of the alley.

He thought she'd give up after the first couple of nights. Nothing happened except they occasionally overheard couples quarreling as they passed through the alley, unaware that their conversation was overheard by two people concealed behind the garbage cans. He thought that she'd be even less enthusiastic when they went to their hiding place the night before garbage pick-up, when the cans were redolent of every noxious odor from discarded cat litter to soiled diapers to food that had passed the date when it was safe for eating. But Kelly didn't complain, even though, by the time he walked her to her car, each was very conscious of the other's aroma.

Kelly didn't complain, but she was feeling the burden of waiting. Lucas was still locked up, and the Krymanskis, united as a clan against the dark looks they received as they passed by, looked after Tia Krymanski as much as she would let them. She wasn't overly fond of her in-laws, Kelly knew, and it galled her to be obliged to them for help.

She showered, washed her hair, and didn't go to bed until she smelled fragrantly of Bath & Body Works Warm Vanilla Sugar Shower Gel. Once in bed, she tried to concentrate on what they'd learned so far.

Nothing. They'd learned nothing because nothing had happened in the alley. Troy forbade her to ask Mrs. Hammond if there had seemed to be any particular pattern in the drug sales. He'd ordered her to leave Mrs. Hammond out of this entirely. If something went wrong, he had said, the two of them would have to deal with it themselves.

She realized that he hadn't tried to sugar-coat the risk, and she supposed she should be appreciative that he allowed her to take part in the stakeouts, however reluctant he had been to agree. She hoped something would happen soon. In the meantime, she would just have to be patient. Sooner or later, the red sports car would return to Daffodil Alley.

Saturday brought snow, unexpected in November. Watching from inside the library as the flakes fell on the ground, Kelly wondered how she and Troy would be able to hide their presence when fallen snow would reveal their footprints. Triple layers of socks and fleece-lined gloves worked well for warmth, but the borough didn't plow the alleys, and as the stores closed early on Saturdays, footprints would be all too visible.

She wasn't surprised to see Troy come into the library a half hour before closing time.

"My weekend off," he answered her quizzical glance.

"Did you sleep in?"

"No, I went out to the Trail to run."

"It's beautiful out there in the snow," she said wistfully.

"It's cold out there in the snow," he said.

"Wimp."

"What do you expect? I was born in Las Vegas."

"You were? I never figured you for a Las Vegas type, somehow."

"I'm not any type. Dad was career military, so we lived everywhere. I stopped by to see if you want to get something to eat after the library closes."

She had planned to go home and take a nap after leaving the library. A couple hours of sleep, maybe a little reading and a leisurely cup of tea before going to Daffodil Alley. She opened her mouth to tell him her plans and was dumfounded to hear herself say that she was really hungry for the pierogis and haluski at the diner.

"What's a girl with a name like Armello know about Polish food?" he teased her when, an hour later, they were seated at a booth in the diner, waiting for their food to be served.

"There's nothing about food that I don't know," she answered. "I love ethnic food festivals. Do you go to them? This whole area was a mini-Europe a century ago. The Italians, the Slovaks, the Poles, the Hungarians . . . they all came over to work in the mills and the mines and the foundries. The Americans conquered with their English language, but the immigrants conquered where it counts, in the food."

"Does everyone in Settler Springs eat here?"

"Pretty much, why?"

"I'm seeing a lot of familiar faces. And they're seeing us."

She looked up, noticed someone she recognized, and waved.

"Is that bad?" she asked. "You don't need to worry. I'm not planning to stake a claim on you."

Troy waited until the waitress had served their meals; roast beef, mashed potatoes and gravy, and carrots for him; pierogies smothered in onions and butter, and haluski for her.

She grinned. "There's nothing like the smell of onions to keep a shy man safe from female machinations."

"I like onions," he said. "I like the smell of them, the taste of 'em . . . so if you ordered the pierogies as a way of making sure that this is just a working dinner, I can't promise that it'll work."

"I didn't figure you for shy," she responded with one of those deft turns of subject that put the navigation of the conversation back under her control. "So tell me, Mr. Police Officer sir, what do we do about the snow?"

They both looked out the window, where the snow that had fallen all day continued as the afternoon darkened.

"We could skip tonight," he said. "I have a fireplace, and this is the perfect night for enjoying a warm fire."

"If I were a dealer," she said, "I'd pick tonight because no one would be paying attention. Except their customers, I suppose."

She clearly had no intention of responding to his flirting. He was starting to understand that Kelly Armello didn't follow, she led. There was a lot more to learn about this self-assured, straightforward woman. In the meantime, back to the working dinner.

He didn't think of addicts as customers, somehow, but he supposed Kelly had a point. Still . . .

"Since you nixed my offer of a warm fire," he said, "I guess we'll have to go with Plan B."

"Which is?"

He held up a key, dangling it from his fingers.

"I rented one of the garages in the Alley," he said.

Kelly knew that there were three joined garages, each with large windows that looked out onto the alley. She hadn't paid much attention to them because no one ever seemed to be going in or coming out of them.

"How did you know that one was vacant?" she asked, impressed.

"I didn't know, until I heard the weather forecast last night. I called the borough secretary, who knows everyone and everything, and told her I need a garage for storage, and did she know of any for rent. My lucky day. I signed the lease this morning after my run."

"Do you need a garage for storage?"

"I just got out of the military," he scoffed. "I travel light. But it'll be a notch or two above freezing inside the garage and we won't get snow on us. We won't be seen. But we'll be able to see if anything is going on, and we can keep a thermos of coffee handy. It won't be anything that AirBnB would advertise, but it'll beat the garbage can circuit."

12

THE SNOWY STAKEOUT

"It never snows this much, this early in November," Kelly said when Troy, who had already arrived at the garage, opened the back entrance to let her in. The snow was still falling; her footprints would soon be covered.

"That's what you think. I had three neighbors who told me that this was nothing compared to the snows of the 1950s, when towns were shut off and the roads closed."

"Not in November," she countered, sitting down on one of the two lawn chairs he'd brought to the garage that morning, along with a few other odds and ends to buttress his claim that he was using the structure for storage. She accepted the thermos cup of coffee gratefully. She was dressed for the cold and the garage was definitely better than being out in the snow, but coffee made a difference.

"Is there anything you don't know?"

"I'm a librarian, remember?"

"You read crime novels like I read the sports pages; you're a weather archive; you're determined to prove that a kid is innocent of murder when the whole town wants him to be guilty; you've been single since you and your ex broke up six months ago and you don't want to get involved in a relationship. What else should I know about you?"

The brightness of the white snow provided a strange, pure illumination but it wasn't easy to see inside the garage. Maybe that made it easier to ask questions like the one he had just posed to Kelly.

"You left out that I run fast," she said.

"I only have that on your say-so. I haven't seen you run."

"Hm. Point made. There is something . . ."

He felt a sense of apprehension. The boyfriend was still in the picture. She was married, not divorced yet. She was involved with someone else. She didn't want to get involved with a cop. She just didn't like him that way.

"I quit going to church when I was sixteen."

"What?" That wasn't the heart-stopping revelation that he'd expected. "Doesn't every kid stop going to church at sixteen?"

"Some do, I guess. But I told my family that I didn't believe in God, that the church was made up of a bunch of hypocrites, that I could worship God—if I wanted to—when I was running on the Trail and I didn't need to be in church on Sunday morning."

"Kelly, if this is your deep, dark secret, I have to tell you that it's pretty low on the teen rebellion scale."

"My grandfather was a minister. I was really close to my grandfather. When he got cancer, he moved in with us and we took care of him. He was dying, but he told me something I've never forgotten. 'Kelly, if you're mad at God about something, let God know. He's big enough to handle it. But if you're just too lazy to decide what you believe, then you're cheating yourself and God too.'" Kelly was quiet for a time.

Troy didn't interrupt. He still didn't understand why this was something that she wanted him to know about her, but it was apparent that it mattered.

"He told me that his dying wish was that I would find God again. In anger, in disappointment, in fear, it didn't matter. Just find God, he said. Look for God, and find Him."

"And?"

"And I did. I was so angry at God when Grandpa got cancer. When he died, we got cards, letters, calls from people he'd known throughout his ministry. That's when I realized that believers don't just listen to sermons, they live them out; those are the people who wear red capes and fly to the rescue. My grandfather had such an impact on so many people's lives. We never knew. He was just Grandpa."

He could sense her smiling even though it was too dark for him to see her expression clearly. "Grandpa's secret identity was that he was just an ordinary, nice guy. But he was a superhero."

"Is this your way of telling me that you're a practicing Christian and that whatever is going to happen between us in the future won't happen unless you decide God is okay with it?"

Kelly stood up and stretched. "You got it," she said, going over to the window to look out. "Troy!"

Troy got up and went to the window.

"There's a car," she whispered. "You see it?"

He saw it. Apparently, a snowy night when most of the town chose to stay inside was a better night for business than Troy would have guessed. The car was covered by the snow, making it impossible to discern its make or its color, but Troy's instincts told him that beneath the snow was the red sports car that Mrs. Hammond had seen.

"I'm going out the back door," he said. "I need to get the license plate number of the car."

"I'm going with you," she said.

"No. There's no reason for two of us to be out there," he said. "You stay in here and see if you recognize anyone going by."

"Troy, I—"

"This isn't the time for the red cape, Kelly," he said. "I'm going to get the license plate number, that's all. You plant yourself at the window and see if you recognize anyone who approaches the car. You know more people in town than I do."

Without waiting for a response, he went to the door at the back end of the garage and went outside. Kelly watched as he vanished into the snow. He had dressed for it, she realized, as she had not, in her dark jeans and dark coat. Troy had on pale gray sweatpants and a white hoodie. Not very warm but designed to let the snow camouflage him if he needed to be outside.

Taking another sip of her coffee, she watched out the window. The snow was still falling, but now she was grateful for it. It would conceal Troy and maybe keep him safe.

Troy, despite his Las Vegas birth, had lived in all climate zones during his life and he knew how to make the snow work for him. He moved quickly, crouching behind bushes, trees, and garbage cans to hide. There was a stretch of parking lot that was out in the open, with no convenient hiding spots, just before he'd reach a point where he could read the license plate. As he crouched behind the garbage can, deciding when to make a move, he heard the sound of another car approaching.

The red car driver was likely to be paying attention to the arriving car. Troy swiftly crossed the parking lot. He was only a few feet away from the red car. Squatting, he made his way alongside the car, below view, so that he could reach the back and see the license plate.

"What are you doing out on a night like this!"

Troy froze. That was Chief Stark's voice. What was the Chief doing out on patrol? The Chief left that to his officers and he wasn't likely to change that habit on a cold, snowy night like this one.

Then he relaxed. The Chief hadn't seen him. He was talking to the driver of the red car."

"Why not?"

The voice was male, young, and cocky. He was inside his car, and Chief Stark was inside a car as well. Not a police car, Troy noted; it was the Chief's own vehicle, a Lexus that was the source of envy for the other officers who struggled to make monthly car payments on their own pick-up trucks and SUVs. Mrs. Stark was an insurance agent; and the insurance business, so the officers joked, must be a good line of work.

"You shouldn't be here," Chief Stark was saying.

"Gotta keep the customers satisfied," the voice said. "Not showing up is bad for business, right?"

The Chief didn't answer at first. Then, "No one will come tonight."

"They'll come," the younger man said. "They have to come."

"Watch yourself," the Chief said.

Then the Lexus drove away; Troy watched it pass by on the other side of the red car. It didn't matter now. While they were talking, he'd carefully made his way to the license plate and memorized it, brushing away enough snow so that he could see. He crawled away from the red car, just as another car approached on the other side.

Mrs. Hammond wasn't a crazy old lady making up stories. She was dead-on in her accusations. Troy waited long enough to listen to the transaction, which was brief and businesslike and apparently satisfactory to both.

He was beginning to feel the cold, but it wasn't anything worse than he'd experienced in Afghanistan during his deployment. He waited; when the next car came, he'd cross the parking lot again and get back to the garage.

Kelly turned from the window as soon as she heard the sound of the door opening.

"Did you get the license plate number?" she asked, pouring a cup of coffee from the thermos. "Did you write it down?"

"I didn't have to," he said. "It's a personalized plate." He drank the entire cup in one swallow, relishing the warm route of the liquid as it traveled inside him. "Fan Solo."

13

THE RED CAR

He knew now, but he needed proof, the kind of proof that could only be provided by the Department of Motor Vehicles. He remembered that, when he first joined the force, there had been a Settler Springs cop who left for the DMV not long after Troy came on board. Nick Bakularov was a good guy, Troy recalled, although he didn't remember much more than the guy's name. But it was worth a try.

Nick remembered him too. "Hey, Troy, how's things? You had a murder last month. It made the TV news."

"Yeah," Troy replied, still soured on the memory of the way the town had turned into an overnight media magnet.

"A Krymanski did it?"

"That's what the state police say."

Nick was alert. "You don't believe it?"

"The Krymanskis aren't in the running for Citizen of the Year, I'll give you that. But they run to petty stuff, mostly. Murder? I doubt it. And the kid is just fourteen."

"In Settler Springs, if there's a crime, it's a Krymanski." Nick sounded bitter. Troy wondered why. He didn't know Nick well enough to ask, but he'd be willing to bet that Nick had a story to tell.

"Yeah, well, that makes it convenient," he said vaguely.

"Convenient for the real criminals."

"That's what I'm starting to find out," Troy responded, his words deliberately suggestive and yet neutral.

"It didn't take you long," Nick said. He sounded reassured.

"Long enough."

"At least you still have your job. Be careful."

"Why?" The question was genuine. He hadn't expected to contact Nick at the DMV to receive a warning.

"You think I'm here because I like working at a desk all day?" That bitter note was back in Nick's inflection. "I'm here because Chief Stark and I had a falling out."

"Over what?" During the time that Troy had been on the force, he hadn't noticed the Chief getting involved in much of anything. He seemed to spend most of his day chatting with the mayor, or making visits to schools and social organizations, or handing off cases to the state police.

"I didn't like the way he was doing some things," Nick said, suddenly cautious. "I called him on it, and here I am."

"You couldn't report him?"

Nick's laugh lacked mirth. "What did you call for, Troy? You want a name for a number?"

"I want confirmation. I have a plate. I need to know who it belongs to."

"Shoot."

"Fan Solo."

Nick sounded disgusted. "I don't even have to look it up and you've been there long enough to know who drives that car. It belongs to Scotty Stark, the Chief's son. That little red rocket that he drives."

"Expensive car for a college kid."

"If Dad can drive a Lexus, Sonny can have an Aston Martin Vanquish. I never understood why he picked Fan Solo for his license plate. The character is Han, isn't it?"

"Maybe Han Solo is trademarked, I don't know. Can you look it up for me?"

"I don't have to—"

"Just look it up, I need to be sure."

There was a pause while Nick began his computer search. "Huh," he said as if the results were a surprise.

"What? It's not the Chief's son?" Troy had been so sure that they had their man and that the pieces were coming together. If he was wrong, he wasn't sure where they went from here.

"Oh, Scotty drives it. But his mother owns it."

"His mother?"

"You know, Lois Stark, the insurance agent?"

"Business must be good," Troy said, repeating the line familiar to him from the others on the force.

"Business must be real good."

He was working the late shift for Leo that night; Leo and his wife had to take their grandkids for a court-mandated counseling assessment in Pittsburgh and it was going to be a long day. Kelly would be at the library until closing time. They hadn't had much of a chance to talk after he'd returned to the garage the night before. They'd stayed there until the stream of cars and pedestrians ended and the red car left. Then they'd waited awhile to make sure no one would see them leaving the garage. Kelly was eager to believe that they'd proven Lucas wasn't guilty, but Troy brought her back to earth when he reminded her that they didn't have proof yet.

Even now, he didn't have proof. But he had a lot more evidence than he'd had when Lucas was first accused of killing Tyra Cardew.

He called Kelly. "How does a late supper sound? I'm working Leo's shift tonight. I can take my break when you get off."

"Okay."

"My place okay? I need to let Arlo out."

He could imagine the smile on her face. "And you don't want anyone to hear us. Okay, Jefferson Street Take-Out it is. I like mushrooms and green peppers on my pizza."

"What about pepperoni?"

"Do you know what's in pepperoni?"

"Is there anything you don't know? No, I don't know what's in pepperoni and I don't want to."

They arrived at his house at the same time, to be met at the door by Arlo, who was so excited by having two people to greet that he wasn't sure which to notice first. Troy submitted to Arlo's enthusiastic welcome before putting him on his leash.

"I can go inside and set the table. It's too cold for you to leave him out long," Kelly said. "Real plates again?"

"Real plates, no booze. I'm working."

When he brought Arlo back inside, the plates were set and coffee was brewing. She noted the pizza—onions on all of it, pepperoni on one half, mushrooms and peppers on the other half—with approval.

"Onions," she said, "the sign of a working meal. What did you find out?"

"The car that Scotty Stark drives is in his mother's name."

"Mrs. Stark? She's the president of the library board. She doesn't pay her overdue fines. We're not allowed to charge her. It's not written anywhere, but it's understood," Kelly said, making a connection that made more sense to her than it did to Troy. "I can see the Lexus that Chief Stark drives, I don't see the Aston Martin, somehow."

"The DMV doesn't lie."

"So, let's see. Mrs. Hammond is right about the drugs and the red car. Scotty Stark is the dealer. Chief Stark knows—"

"We think he knows. We didn't hear him say anything that specifically ties his son to the drug dealing."

"They both mentioned customers."

"But not drugs. Scotty Stark could be scalping hockey tickets for all we know. Maybe he likes to come home from school and meet his old friends in Daffodil Alley, one at a time. Kelly, we can't fabricate evidence that we don't have. What we do have is proof that Mrs. Hammond isn't making it up when she said that she sees a red sports car in Daffodil Alley on a regular basis. She and Lucas both saw the car the night of the murder."

"It's something, isn't it?"

Troy smiled. "It's something," he agreed.

Kelly stretched in her chair. "I feel a lot better now," she said.

"You ought to feel like you can't move after eating four pieces of pizza."

"You had four, too."

"I'm six feet, two inches," he retorted.

"I'm tall for my gender. What do we do now?"

"You're going to contact Lucas's lawyer and tell him what you know."

"You mean it?" she asked, her eyes bright. "You're going to let me do that?"

"It's your turn to wear the red cape."

14

THE CASE IS SOLVED

Lucas was just glad to be home, even if it meant that Mom was hovering over him as if she couldn't bear to let him out of her sight. His sisters were the same, even the twins, who let him choose the program he wanted to watch on television. Marissa baked chocolate chip cookies for him, and Carrie let him use her iPad. Minute by minute, as he sat in the crowded kitchen with his family, the memories of his stay in the detention center began to fade.

Mom was insisting that he would need to see a counselor. He didn't want to, but she said it would be covered by health insurance and he wasn't to worry about the expense. She wanted to make sure that when he returned to school after Christmas break, he was ready to return.

"I'm innocent," he answered, holding up his plate so that Mom could put more stuffed cabbages on it. "Everyone knows it now."

"Police Chief Stark is on leave from the police force," Carrie said.

"He didn't have much choice," Mrs. Krymanski declared. "His son murdered that girl and tried to make you take the blame. If that girl's parents hadn't raised a fuss, you might have gone to prison."

"I wonder what made them stir things up," Carrie pondered. "They didn't do much at first."

"I suppose they were in shock," her mother said. "Losing a daughter to murder would be too horrible to think about. Then, I suppose they started to ask questions themselves and they realized that nothing added up."

"It's a good thing they have money," Carrie said. "They got attention when they said that the investigation wasn't complete."

"No one listened to us when we said that Lucas was innocent," Marissa recalled.

"And then, when that old lady came forward and said she'd seen the car in the alley that night," Carrie continued. "That proved that Lucas was telling the truth."

"Lucas, you're going to carry her trash out for her every week on trash night," his mother said. "Carrie, I want you to do her grocery shopping for her. Lucas can carry the bags up for you."

Neither of her offspring complained.

"What can I do?" Marissa asked.

"Bake cookies for her. Miss Armello knows her from the library; she said she loves cookies."

"What about us?" Alexa wanted to know.

"I'll find something," Mrs. Krymanski said forcefully. "I'm sure there are things that you can do to help."

"I just don't understand why it took as long as it did. Even if Officer Kennedy says it didn't really take that long, once things started moving."

"It felt like a long time to me," Lucas said darkly. "I don't ever want to end up in that place again."

"Stay out of trouble," his mother admonished, "and you won't have to. And that goes for the rest of you," she said, encircling her brood with a warning look.

"Lucas is the only one who gets into trouble," Marissa pointed out. "Except for when Carrie got into a fight with that girl."

Lucas stared at his oldest sister. He hadn't heard that story. "You got into a fight?"

"Some girl was saying things about you," Carrie said in an off-handed manner. "She was getting on my nerves."

"The school called the police," Madison relayed the story with zest, now that the episode was over, and with it, the fear of an uncertain and threatening time in their family. "Officer Kennedy brought her home in the police car."

"I'll bet you were grounded for a month!" Lucas said, thrilled at the prospect of his sister's sentence.

His sister examined her nails. "No," she said. "Mom didn't punish me."

Lucas was about to protest the unfairness of the treatment she had received compared to his usual fate, when the doorbell rang. Mrs. Krymanski went to answer it. Even though Lucas was home and the real murderer, Scotty Stark, had been arrested, she was vigilant about the safety of the family. No one was to talk to the press, she told her children.

They knew she meant it, but no one balked at the rule. They'd had enough attention. They wanted to be left alone.

"Officer Kennedy! Miss Armello! Come on in. We're eating supper and there's plenty. Join us."

It was a command, not an invitation and Carrie pulled two chairs to the table while Marissa got plates and the twins finished the table settings. By the time the guests were in the dining room, their places were ready.

"We didn't mean to interrupt your supper," Kelly said. "We just wanted to stop by and see how Lucas is doing, now that he's been home for a few days."

"He's doing fine, and he'll be able to finish doing his community service hours," Mrs. Krymanski said.

"Good," Kelly smiled at Lucas. "We're getting everything ready for the kids' Christmas program this weekend and we could use an extra pair of hands. Officer Kennedy is going to help, too."

"I think you and I will be doing the heavy lifting, Lucas," Troy said. "I hope you're up to it."

Lucas nodded. "Miss Armello moves all the tables out of the library," he said. "So, there's plenty of room for Santa Claus," he said, giving Troy a meaningful look that warned him to play along, because there were believers present.

"Do you want me to bake anything for the Christmas program?" Marissa offered as she handed Kelly the casserole dish with stuffed cabbages packed aromatically inside.

Kelly put three on her plate and passed the dish to Troy. "If you can," she said. "We'll have lunch with Santa after he gives out the toys. How about brownies?"

"She makes good brownies," Lucas admitted, unused to finding a reason to praise the sister who was closest to him in age. "As long as they have frosting on them."

"They'll have frosting on them, but they aren't for you, they're for the kids."

"What about the helpers?" Troy asked. "Can't we have brownies?"

The conversation continued in that vein while they were eating. When the meal was finished, Mrs. Krymanski told her kids to clear the table and clean up the kitchen. She wanted to talk to Officer Kennedy and Miss Armello in private.

She led them to a small room that appeared to serve as a catch-all for winter coats and boots, sports equipment, lawn furniture, and various items. She closed the door and sat down, indicating that they should do the same.

"It's impossible to find any privacy in this house," she said. "But I want to know if Lucas is safe now."

"From arrest, you mean?" Troy asked. "He is. Scott Stark confessed. He picked Tyra Cardew up at the shopping plaza to take her to a Halloween party, just like she had told her father. But that's when she told him she was pregnant. They got into a fight. He said she wouldn't stop crying. He strangled her . . . dropped her body in the alley and took off. The tenant in the upstairs apartment saw the car. She didn't get a license number, but she'd seen the car there before. It seems that Scott Stark was a drug dealer in town. No one ever asked how he was able to afford such an expensive car."

"His parents didn't ask?" Mrs. Krymanski asked in disbelief.

Chief of Police Roger Stark was on leave and likely to resign from the force because he was currently under investigation for involvement in local drug trafficking. But that wasn't widely known, and Troy wasn't going to divulge the information. The town was still stunned from the news that a Stark, not a Krymanski, was the villain in this unexpected turn of events and it would take time before the council would be able to come to grips with the change in fortunes. In the meantime, Leo Page was acting chief of police.

Kelly and Troy said goodbye and left the house.

"He'll be all right," Troy said. "He has a solid family behind him. I'm not saying he'll stay out of trouble, but he'll be all right."

Kelly slid her gloved hand into Troy's hand. He looked at her in surprise as they walked down the street. Christmas was underway. The streets were decorated. People were lining up at the post office to mail presents and cards. It was late afternoon.

"Are we out in the open now?" he asked, squeezing her hand.

"I figured your hands are cold," she answered. "I'm helping keep them warm. Besides, there's nothing to hide."

"No one knows that we were involved," he said. "Mrs. Hammond spoke up when the DA's office called her, and once Mr. Cardew started kicking up the dust, everything moved pretty quickly."

"I didn't want you to be at risk in the police department, if anyone thought that you were giving away information. People in small towns have long memories."

"Not too long, I hope. I don't want people to remember that Lucas was accused of the murder."

"They're going to remember that Scotty Stark is a killer," she said.

He didn't argue with her prediction. A girl was dead, and the killer was caught. The justice that she'd hoped for had been won.

"How about a date?" he said.

"A date?"

"If we're not hiding anymore, why not come out in the open?"

"We weren't hiding," she said with dignity. "We had dinner a few times."

"How about dinner and a movie? Or take-out and Nexflix?"

"How about a run on the Trail this weekend?"

He was ready to answer when they both heard the sound of a window opening above them.

"Mrs. Hammond!" Kelly greeted. "What are you doing with your windows open in this weather? It's only twenty degrees out!"

"I wanted to invite you two to dinner," the old lady said as she beamed down at them. "I'm putting my tree up this weekend and I could use some help."

"We'd love to," Kelly replied. "What are you having?"

Mrs. Hammond laughed. "Oh, I haven't decided yet."

"Make sure it has lots of onions," Troy called up. "We work better with onions."

THANK YOU FOR CHOOSING A PUREREAD BOOK!

We hope you enjoyed the story, and as a way to thank you for choosing PureRead we'd like to send you this free Special Edition Cozy, and other fun reader rewards...

Click Here to download your free Cozy Mystery
PureRead.com/cozy

Thanks again for reading.

See you soon!

If you loved this story why not continue straight away
with other books in the series?

Murder Wears A Mask

Murder Casts a Shadow

Murder Plans The Menu

Murder Wears a Medal

Murder Is A Smoking Gun

Murder Has a Heart

OR READ THE COMPLETE BOXSET!

Start Reading On Amazon Now

OUR GIFT TO YOU

AS A WAY TO SAY THANK YOU WE WOULD
LOVE TO SEND YOU THIS SPECIAL EDITION
COZY MYSTERY FREE OF CHARGE.

Our Reader List is 100% FREE

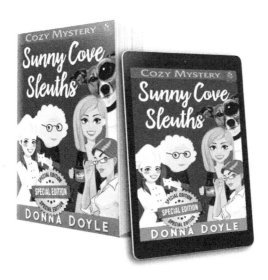

Click Here to download your free Cozy Mystery
PureRead.com/cozy

At PureRead we publish books you can trust. Great tales without smut or swearing, but with all of the mystery and romance you expect from a great story.

Be the first to know when we release new books, take part in our fun competitions, and get surprise free books in your inbox by signing up to our Reader list.

As a thank you you'll receive this exclusive Special Edition Cozy available only to our subscribers...

Click Here to download your free Cozy Mystery
PureRead.com/cozy

Thanks again for reading.
See you soon!

Made in the USA
Coppell, TX
23 September 2023